BULLET BAIT

There had been five of them, five merciless killers, who took Skye Fargo and Clare Standish captive. They planned killing Skye fast. And before they finished with Clare, she would wish she were dead.

Now just one of them, their leader, was left, holed up in a niche in a tall rock.

"Work your way to the horses," Skye told Clare. "Ride the Ovaro. Take off along the side where he can't see you from the niche."

By now the headstrong female was obeying Skye. As she rode off, a figure emerged from the niche and brought his rifle up to fire at her. Fargo's shot exploded first and the side of the man's head seemed to vanish.

That should have been the end of the killing Clare had caused. But it was only the beginning. . . .

THE
TEXAS TRAIN

by
Jon Sharpe

A SIGNET BOOK

NEW AMERICAN LIBRARY

A DIVISION OF PENGUIN BOOKS USA INC.

NAL BOOKS ARE AVAILABLE AT QUANTITY DISCOUNTS
WHEN USED TO PROMOTE PRODUCTS OR SERVICES.
FOR INFORMATION PLEASE WRITE TO PREMIUM MARKETING DIVISION.
NEW AMERICAN LIBRARY. 1633 BROADWAY.
NEW YORK. NEW YORK 10019.

The first chapter of this book previously appeared in
Death's Caravan, the ninety-second volume in this series.

SIGNET TRADEMARK REG. U.S. PAT. OFF. AND FOREIGN COUNTRIES
REGISTERED TRADEMARK—MARCA REGISTRADA
HECHO EN DRESDEN. TN. USA

SIGNET, SIGNET CLASSIC, MENTOR, ONYX, PLUME, MERIDIAN and NAL BOOKS are published by New American Library, a division of Penguin Books USA Inc., 1633 Broadway, New York, New York 10019

First Printing, September, 1989

1 2 3 4 5 6 7 8 9

PRINTED IN THE UNITED STATES OF AMERICA

The Trailsman

Beginnings . . . they bend the tree and they mark the man. Skye Fargo was born when he was eighteen. Terror was his midwife, vengeance his first cry. Killing spawned Skye Fargo, ruthless, cold-blooded murder. Out of the acrid smoke of gunpowder still hanging in the air, he rose, cried out a promise never forgotten.

The Trailsman, they began to call him, all across the West: searcher, scout, hunter, the man who could see where others only looked, his skills for hire but not his soul, the man who lived each day to the fullest, yet trailed each tomorrow. Skye Fargo, the Trailsman, the seeker who could take the wildness of a land and the wanting of a woman and make them his own.

*Texas, 1859, just south
of the Concho River,
where the long shadow of
the Alamo still lingered . . .*

1

The big man's lake-blue eyes peered down at the flat land below where the train slowly chugged its way beneath the cloudless, sun-swept sky. There were a hundred rifle-carrying men riding the four cars, and alone, all by himself, he was going to attack that train.

Skye Fargo repeated the words again inside himself as he had done a dozen times over the last hour, as though he were still trying to make himself believe it. An oath escaped his lips with the deep breath he took, and his powerfully muscled shoulders lifted in a half-shrug. What was he doing here? he asked himself. How did he let himself get talked into this suicidal, damn-fool idea? How had he taken leave of his senses? But then he'd asked himself the same questions for the past three days as he rode across the Texas country-side and made ready for this moment.

He had taken a hell of a lot of damn-fool jobs over the years, but this had to be the granddaddy of them all. But he was here, even though he was still having trouble believing it. The price of hot loins and an active conscience. Either was a terrible burden on a man. Together they were a millstone around his neck. Or was it around something else? The little train continued its slow chugging, and Fargo let the days flash backward as he waited.

He'd been in Possum Kingdom, north of Abilene, a hot, bustling little town where he'd finished breaking trail for the Symonds brothers herd, all the way from the Kansas border. It had been a job too long, too hard, and for too little money, but that was how they turned out sometimes. The Aapche had been scarce—he'd been grateful for that—and when it was finished, he'd celebrated with too much bourbon. But that, too, had ended. He was about to leave Possum Kingdom, watering the magnificent Ovaro at the town trough for the ride back north, when the young woman appeared at his elbow.

He stared at her for a long moment. In Possum Kingdom she was not unlike a starflower in a bog, her beauty startling, unexpected and misplaced. He took in gray eyes in an even-featured face, high cheek-bones, a face of commanding attractiveness under soft brown hair. Her dark-green dress enclosed a slender figure, and the square-cut neckline let the tops of beautifully full breasts rise into view.

"Skye Fargo, the Trailsman," she said softly, a statement not a question.

"Bull's-eye, the big man said. "Though I didn't know I was wearing a name tag."

"Riding, not wearing," she said with a smile and a glance at the striking Ovaro still drinking from the trough.

"That all?" Fargo asked, though the horse had been his identity often enough.

"No. I was informed that you were breaking trail for the Symonds herd and that you'd end up here," she said, her words uttered with cool, crisp diction. "I must talk to you. I've a room at the inn. Will you go with me, please? It's just down the street."

"Honey, I'd go with you if it was in Mexico," Fargo said. He swung in beside her as she set off down the street. She walked with a smooth motion that hardly moved her breasts inside the square-necked dress, he noted.

The Possum Kingdom Inn was the most respectable building in town and the only one with a fresh coat of paint on it. He followed the young woman down a ground-floor hallway. She used her room key to open a door and he went in after her, his lake-blue eyes scanning the room at once. One closet, its door open, he saw, the rest of the room ordinary enough: a single bed and a worn dresser with a big white porcelain washbasin on top of it.

The young woman closed the door and turned to him, a cool amusement in her gray eyes. "I expect you're curious about this," she said.

"That's the right word, honey," Fargo said. "What's all this about?"

"It's about hiring you," the young woman said.

"You want to hire me?" Fargo questioned with a frown.

"No, not me. I was sent by someone to hire you," she answered.

"Who are you?"

"Jill Foster," she said. "Herbert S.andish sent me to hire you for him."

"Who the hell is Herbert Standish?"

"A very wealthy man, a very determined man, a very ruthless man."

"Why didn't he come hire me himself?" Fargo frowned.

"He expected you'd ask that."

"That's one for him. Now, answer the question," Fargo said, a trace of annoyance coming into his voice.

"He thought I'd do a much better job of convincing you to take the job than he would," Jill said.

Fargo half-smiled as his eyes went over the young woman again. "He could be right, there," he remarked. "What does Herbert Standish want to hire me for?" Fargo asked.

"He wants you to take his daughter off a train." The young woman turned to a small suitcase at the edge of the bed.

"That doesn't take a trailsman," Fargo said.

"That part will come later," Jill said as she reached into the suitcase and drew out a sheaf of new, crisp bills and put them on top of the dresser in front of him. "There's two thousand dollars there, with two thousand more when you finish the job."

Fargo stared at the money and heard the low whistle that escaped his lips. "That's a lot of convincing money. All to take his daughter off a train?"

"He wants his daughter off that train real bad," Jill Foster said, and Fargo's smile was chiding tolerance.

"I've been around too long. No more sweet talk. What's the catch?"

"There is a problem," she said casually. "There will be a hundred armed guards on the train."

Fargo felt his eyebrows arch. "A hundred armed guards?" he echoed. "Yes, I guess you could call that a problem?"

"They're soldiers of the Mexican army," she said, and Fargo knew his brows arched still further.

"A hundred soldiers of the Mexican army up here in Texas?" He frowned. "You've got to be kidding. That'd cause another damn war?"

"That's why they'll all be dressed in ordinary clothes. But they're soldiers of the Mexican army."

"And I'm supposed to go up there all by myself and take the girl," Fargo muttered. "All that money is suicide pay, honey."

"No. Standish is convinced you're the one man who can pull it off. You've a reputation for doing things other men can't do," Jill said.

"I've done a few but I'm no damn magician."

"It's an awful lot of money to turn down, Fargo," she said with a glance at the sheaf of bills.

12

"It is, but then, I can't spend much of it dead, can I?" the big man answered.

Her shrug was a dismissal of his remark. "Mr. Standish is convinced you won't let that happen," she said.

Fargo appraised Jill Foster and saw her cool, composed manner remained intact, her very attractive face showing only a calm confidence. "Tell me, honey, why doesn't Standish hire his own army of gunhands to attack the train and take the girl?" Fargo asked.

"He figured you'd ask that," Jill said. "He gave me two reasons. First, he'd have no advantage of surprise if he hired a hundred gunhands. Word would get out. Somebody would talk and they'd be ready and waiting on the train. Second, that'd bring on the kind of wild battle that could get the girl killed by any of a thousand stray bullets. He won't risk that."

Fargo turned the answer in his mind and had to agree with Standish's thinking. "He have any ideas on how one man can do what a hundred can't?" he asked with an edge of sarcasm.

"Surprise. Find a way to stop the train. Then find a way to get the girl off. They won't be expecting one man. They'll be looking for an attacking force. He feels one man has the only chance," Jill said.

Fargo turned the answer in his mind and allowed a wry smile. "He could be right, there, but not this man, honey," he answered. "As a gambling man I knew used to say, I don't like the cards and I don't like the odds. Tell Mr. Standish to keep his money and find a new boy."

"He expected you might say that," Jill answered. "It's known that money doesn't carry the weight with you that it does with most men."

"True enough, especially where my neck is concerned," Fargo said.

"That's another reason why Mr. Standish sent me to

convince you instead of himself," Jill Foster said, her face remaining coolly unsmiling. But her hand went to the top button of the dress, pulled it open, and went down to the next. Fargo realized his mouth had fallen open as she unbuttoned the entire dress, bent forward gracefully, and stepped from it. She pulled off her bloomers and turned to face him, gloriously naked.

He closed his mouth, licking the dryness from his lips as he stared at her. She had smooth, round shoulders, with prominent collarbones below. Her lovely breasts were beautifully tipped by pink nipples set in the center of darker pink circles. A lean rib cage curved down to a smooth abdomen, and narrow hips, and a flat belly adorned with a dark triangle of modest curliness. Her legs were shaped in a lean, angular line with thin calves.

But she was all waiting and throbbing, and she looked back at him with a kind of defiance in her eyes, defiance and determination and perhaps pride. He felt the stirring inside him, impossible to deny. But the frown dug into his brow on the outside, the astonishment into his gut on the inside. She was no saloon girl. He'd have caught that in her face and manner. Yet she was there naked before him, meeting his stare with the controlled throbbing in her eyes. "I'll be damned," Fargo breathed. "You're giving a new meaning to the word 'convincing,' I'll say that for you."

"I hope so. The money's only part of it, now. I'm the rest," she said. "Agree to get the girl from the train and you have me and the money."

Fargo searched her face. "What's this Standish paying you for this?"

"That's not important. It's not your concern. I'm here for you, that's all you need know," she said. Defiant pride flared in her gray eyes as dots of color spread in her cheeks. "I've never done this for anyone else, not like this, if that means anything to you," she added.

"It might, under different circumstances," Fargo said, and watched the furrow slide across her brow.

"What does that mean?"

"It means the answer's still no."

Jill Foster's eyes widened. "You can't mean that," she murmured, apprehension coming into her voice.

"Sorry, honey," Fargo said.

She blinked, swallowing hard as something between dismay and dejection flashed through her face. She took a step back, the full-cupped breasts swaying gently, and he felt the surge inside him at the waiting, willing loveliness of her. He swore inwardly as he fought down the urge to take her. She halted, spun suddenly, scooped up the dress, and held it to her protectively.

"Go. Get out of here," she murmured, not looking at him, and he caught the waver in her voice.

"Look, it's nothing personal," he offered. "I mean, it's nothing to do with you." He swore silently as he heard himself stumbling over words. "You could be Cleopatra and Helen of Troy rolled into one and it'd still be no," he managed to say.

She sank down on the edge of the bed, the dress held modestly over her. "Go, just go, please," she said, and the sob in her voice was definite now.

He took a step toward her, reached out, closed one hand around her shoulder, and felt the smooth warmth of her. She looked up and he saw the tear stains on her cheeks. "Don't take it so hard. You sure improved the cards, but the odds are the same. I told you, it's nothing to do with you."

"I understand. I'm not feeling rejected," she murmured, her voice small.

"You could fool me," Fargo said.

Her gray eyes were round as she looked up at him,

another tear sliding down her cheek. "You asked what Standish was paying me to do this," she said, and swallowed a sob. "He's holding my little sister. He told me not to bother coming back for her if I didn't get you to agree."

Fargo frowned at her. "Jesus, what kind of bastard is he?"

"I told you, a very clever and a very ruthless one," Jill Foster answered. She wiped the back of one hand across her eyes and rose to her feet, the dress still held protectively to her, and she allowed only a glimpse of one thigh to show. "I can't blame you for refusing. I tried. I did everything he told me to do," she said, more to herself than him.

"That doesn't usually count with that kind of man."

Her smile was bitter as her gray eyes met his stare. "No, I don't expect it will," she said, and her eyes stayed on him. "I hated doing this, the very thought of it sickened me. But when I finally met you, I decided maybe it wouldn't be as bad as I was afraid it would be. But that doesn't matter much now, does it?"

The cool determination had vanished, leaving a waiflike, helplessness surrounding her. Fargo swore inwardly. "What are you going to do now?" he asked.

Her round, bare shoulders offered a disconsolate shrug. "Go back. Try to get my sister. It's all I can do, and I don't have much hope for that," she answered.

Fargo felt the grimness stabbing hard at him and he realized that not only was she desirable but her helpless had added a new, even more appealing dimension to her. "What happens if I try and don't get the girl? Will that get your sister and you off the hook?" he asked. Fargo saw the flare of hope come into her gray eyes even as she continued to frown at him.

"You mean that?" she asked as she peered hard at him. "You saying you'll do it?"

"For your little sister." He nodded, and still holding the dress to her, she circled his neck with one arm and clung to him for a long moment. When she stepped back, her eyes were shining and gratitude had replaced the bitterness in her smile.

"Thank you, Fargo," she said. "Thank you."

"Hell, I've tried damn-fool things before, made them work, sometimes," he grumbled. "I guess I can try one more." He let a sigh escape his lips as he started to turn away. "You can get dressed."

The single word came to him, softly yet firmly. "No."

He turned back to her, a furrow on his brow, to see her standing with the dress still held protectively in front of her. "I can't let you do that without playing my part through. That wouldn't be fair. I made my agreements, with Herbert Standish and with myself. I won't go back on them. Not to you, either. I came as part of the offer. I won't go back on that," Jill Foster said.

Her hand opened and the dress fell to the floor. She stood before him again with her waiting, naked loveliness, and he felt the surging inside him at once. It was no time for words. He stepped toward her and began to pull off clothes; she waited, arms half-outstretched, her eyes watching as he shed the last of his garments.

He knew he was already throbbing with desire, already erect and ready. Jill Foster's eyes widened in appreciative anticipation, and then he was against her, pressing himself to the curly triangle.

"Oh, oh, God," she murmured, sinking back onto the bed.

His mouth found hers, her lips open, wanting, her tongue a warm softness darting against him. His mouth stayed on her sweetness and his hands found the two beautifully cupped breasts, rubbed the pink tips, and felt their soft firmness rise at his touch.

17

"Oh, ooooh, yes," Jill breathed, and her arms came up, her hands clasping his head as she pulled his lips to her breast and cried out at the touch. She pushed up, thrusting the soft mound up into his mouth, moaning as he took it, gently pulled, letting his tongue caress. He moved his hips, and his organ pushed through the curly, soft-wire nap; he dropped downward and touched the softness of her inner thighs.

"Aaaaaah," Jill gasped, and Fargo felt her thighs lift, fall open. He moved his torso, slid forward, and touched her dark wetness. He heard her half-scream of delight as he moved forward, paused, moved again, and her cry curled into the air. Her lean thighs came around his waist, pressed, and Jill Foster began to make soft moaning sounds as she moved with him. He felt the warm wetness envelop him, touching, clinging, coating—liquescent ecstasy—and the senses took command, the flesh making its own demands, passion a sweet master. He felt himself move with the young woman as she thrust and pumped with him.

"Yes, yes, oh, my, oh, oh . . . aaaaah," she cried out, and the low moaning sounds turned higher, became soft gasps, each wrapped in its own ecstasy. He smothered his face into the full softness of her beautifully cupped breasts, one pink tip pressing into the corner of his closed eye. Her hands dug into his back and he felt her grow tense, her body responding, signaling, heralding the explosion of evanescent ecstasy, of timelessness compressed into a moment where nothing else but itself existed.

"Now! Now! *Now*," Jill Foster screamed, and she clutched at him as he felt the moment sweep through him. He was with her in oneness, immersed in her very being as her lingering cry reverberated around him and her lean legs quivered and held tight against him. His mouth was still holding one lovely breast when he felt her body go limp, her legs fall away, and the soft sigh escape her lips.

But she held his head against her, murmuring tiny sounds until he finally withdrew and lay beside her. She nestled against him and let silence and the warm aftermath of passion embrace her until she finally lifted herself onto one elbow, her finger tracing a line against his muscled chest. "I won't be going back till morning," she murmured.

"Good," he said, and her small smile quickly translated itself into her hands moving softly across his body. She traced invisible lines over his muscled frame, and he let her do as she wished, responding to her subtle and not-so-subtle messages of the flesh. The night had come when she screamed again and gasped out her paean to ecstasy. She curled against him when it was finished, and slept in his arms until he woke with the morning's light, moved, and slid from the bed.

He used the porcelain basin to wash and was almost dressed when Jill woke, stretched, and looked provocatively beautiful. He handed her the washcloth by the basin and she washed while he finished dressing. She threw a shawl around her shoulders that let the pink tips of her breasts poke through with insouciant boldness.

Fargo sat down at the other side of the bed from her and fought away the urges that pushed at him. "Got some questions for you, Jill," he said. "A lot still needs answering."

"I'll try. I don't know much more than I've told you," she said.

"Why are a hundred disguised soldiers of the Mexican army bringing this girl into Texas by railroad?" he asked.

"I asked about that, and was told it was none of my business," Jill said.

"Who was she in Mexico in the first place?"

"Standish told me his wife ran away with a Mexican general a few years back and took the girl with her," Jill said. "As for the railroad, it's a little spur line that runs a few hundred miles north from Laredo."

"I know it. A few rich Texans put it together, thought it'd be a great idea to have their own railroad," Fargo said. "Only it's a joke as a railroad and a disaster as business venture." He watched Jill as she finished dressing and vigorously combed her brown hair. She turned and took the money from the dresser and handed it to him. "One last thing," he said as he put the money into his pocket. "If I get the girl, what do I do with her?"

She smiled. "You saved the most important question for last," Jill said. "You're to take her west to a town called Jonah. It's at the foot of the Ketchum Mountains. Standish will be there to meet you."

"I guess that's it, then, with a hell of a lot of questions hanging fire," Fargo said, and his eyes met Jill's steady gaze. "Will you be doing anything more for Standish?"

"No, never," she said.

"Maybe we'll meet up again."

"That's not likely. I'm going east," the young woman said, and rested one hand on his chest. "But I won't be forgetting this. It could've been so awful and you made it so wonderful."

"I won't be forgetting it either, and I hope for the same reasons," Fargo said grimly.

Jill Foster kissed him and stepped back, her gray eyes coolly contained once again as he hurried from the room . . .

Skye Fargo let the pictures and remembrances snap from his mind. Warm lips and willing arms vanished, and his lake-blue eyes narrowed as he stared down at the little train. It had made its chugging, slow way to the edge of the high land. Fargo looked down from beneath a black oak. The train would be passing under the line of rocks where he waited . . . A grim grunt escaped his lips. It was time to make the first move, time to begin the attack. He spurred the pinto along the ledge of the rocks, a glorious army of one.

2

Fargo gazed down from the top of the tall rock formation. Below, the track passed between the two high rock-lined walls. The train had come into sight, still in open land, puffing slowly along, pulled by a small engine with a short cowcatcher, a tall black smokestack, and a tender coupled close behind. Two flatbed cars followed the engine tender, both covered with the Mexican soldiers who were clothed mostly in ponchos and serapes. The men sat crowded shoulder-to-shoulder. A closed passenger car followed, curtains drawn over the four windows in it. An armed guard was positioned on both the front and rear platforms of the car, Fargo noted. The girl would be in there, he grunted, perhaps with more armed guards inside. Perhaps not, though. He'd wrestle with that when the time came. Two horse cars made up the rest of the train, altogether far too heavy a load for the little engine that puffed clouds of black smoke as it strained to pull its way over the tracks.

The afternoon was starting to draw to a close and Fargo had spent the entire morning in preparation for this moment. It would take the engine another five minutes to enter the narrow passage between the two tall rock formations. He turned the Ovaro along the edge of the rocks, increasing the distance between himself and the slowly chugging train below. A trading post just outside Possum Kingdom had sold him the

He dismounted in the crevice as night began to push the twilight aside. The soldiers below built two fires—one at the front of the engine, the other alongside the flatbed cars—and as no attack came, they decided the slide had been the result of natural causes. Even from where he watched, he could see the men relax, move about more freely, and settle down to eat supper.

But the officer in charge was a prudent man, Fargo saw, and he smiled grimly as six sentries were set out along the length of the train on both sides. They were positioned with entirely too much space between each man.

Fargo sat down on the rocks and let the night deepen. Below, the men finished their meal and began to climb back onto the flatbed cars. Soon they were asleep, the long, dark shape of the train outlined by the two fires. Finally Fargo climbed back onto the Ovaro and slowly started down the crevice through the rock.

A half-moon hung tilted in the sky when he reached the bottom of the crevice. He halted, dismounted again, and left the horse inside the narrow passageway. He stepped from the crevice, stayed flattened against the rocks, and moved downward until he was opposite the first of the horse cars that made up the rear of the train.

The nearest sentry was a good twenty yards away, the man leaning against his rifle and altogether relaxed. Fargo dropped into a low crouch as he moved into the open. He crossed the distance to the horse car in a dozen long, loping strides and halted against the black shadows of the horse car, scanned the length of the train, and saw the sentry hadn't moved. Satisfied, Fargo turned and began to pull himself up at the rear of the car on the iron bars that ran ladderlike up to the roof.

Once on the roof, the Trailsman flattened himself and crawled on his stomach. He passed the figure of the sentry below and finally reached the other end of the car. The horses sensed him and made nervous sounds, but they had been doing that since the explosion and no one below paid any attention.

Poised at the end of the roof of the car, Fargo stretched his neck forward just far enough to be able to peer down at the rear platform of the closed passenger car. The sentry there was still in place, he saw, but he was no more alert than the one outside; the man leaned back against the car, his eyes more closed than open.

Still keeping flat, Fargo turned his body around on the roof of the car, found the iron ladder with one foot, and started to climb down the rungs, each descending step a silent pause. The sentry was almost directly beneath him on the platform of the passenger car.

Fargo's lips drew back in a grimace, and he cursed silently. He was in no position to reach his gun, and if the guard came awake and looked up, it would all be over: the silence, the surprise, and his life.

Yet Fargo had to go down another two steps to be close enough. Not daring to breathe, he lowered himself again on the iron brackets. He halted again, his eyes on the sentry. One more step, he murmured inwardly, and he slowly, silently turned his body so that he faced the sentry as he descended the last step, his hands raised over his head to cling to the iron brackets.

Close enough now, the Trailsman drew his leg up, measured distance, and exploding the strength of his tightly drawn muscles, hurled a tremendous kick at the sentry. His foot caught the man on the jaw and the sentry's head flew back even as he crumpled into a heap on the platform of the car.

Fargo was leaping down before the man hit the floor, and caught the rifle in one hand before it fell with a loud clatter. He pushed the sentry to the side of the platform with his foot and faced the closed door to the car. Drawing the big, powerful Colt, he used his left hand to slowly turn the door handle. If there were guards inside the car, it would all come down to a shoot-out inside and another outside when he tried to run with the girl. Not much chance of success.

His lips a thin line, Fargo felt the latch give and the door come open. He pushed it inward, not more than an inch, enough to press one eye to the crack and see into the car. No guards, he breathed in relief. In fact, the car seemed empty until suddenly the girl stepped into view from one side. She was tall, with pale lemon hair that hung below her shoulders. She turned, and he saw a pastel face, everything delicately colored, eyebrows blond, eyes a light gray, cream-colored skin with a faint rosy tint in the smooth cheeks, lips a faint pink—a face delicate yet with strength in the line of her jaw and unquestionably attractive in its own dulcet way.

But a furrow creased his brow. Fargo had expected a young child, perhaps ten or twelve years old. Jill Foster had never mentioned age, only that Standish wanted his daughter taken from the train, and Fargo uttered a silent snort at himself. He'd certainly jumped to conclusions, he reprimanded himself as his eyes took in the rest of the young woman. She wore a white cotton nightgown that hid most of the rest of her, but the folds of the garment touched legs that were plainly long.

The Colt still in his hand, Fargo pushed the door open, darted into the room, and slammed the door shut behind him.

The young woman spun in surprise, a frown darkening the light gray eyes. "Who are you?" she asked, more surprise than fear in her voice.

"Somebody who's come to take you out of here," he said, and saw the flash of hope come to her eyes.

"Mother sent you?" she asked.

"No, your father. I'm taking you to him," Fargo said. He saw the light vanish from her eyes as a frown creased her smooth brow.

"Like hell you are," she snapped, whirled, and dashed for the window.

Fargo took a split second to recover from his surprise, but he managed to reach the window just as she reached for the drawn curtains. He seized her wrist and pulled her hand back as he swung her around. "No, dammit, you'll get us all killed," he rasped.

"Not all of us. Just you," she hissed, brought her other hand around in a swinging arc to rake his face with her nails.

Fargo ducked away from the blow, dropped the Colt into its holster to free his other hand, and swung her in a half-circle. She half-stumbled into one of the chairs in the car and he moved toward her again.

"What's wrong with you, dammit?" he hissed.

"Get a better story, liar," she flung back.

He jumped away from a kick aimed at his groin. Little Miss Pastel Delicacy could be anything but delicate. She leapt from the chair, twisted away from his reach, and half-fell, the nightgown rising up to reveal one long, beautifully curved leg. He caught her by the shoulders as she tried to reach the door at the other end of the car; he spun her around and pulled away from another raking blow. His own punch was short, landing in the pit of her stomach, and she went down on her knees gasping for breath. He yanked her head up by her lemon-blond hair and saw the fury in her eyes.

"Now, look here, dammit! I don't know what your problem is and I don't give a damn, but you're coming with me," he said. "I've been paid to take you to Herb Standish and that's where you're going."

"Damn liar," she hissed as her breath returned.

"You can come along nicely or I'll carry you out of here unconscious," Fargo said, and her eyes stared back as she read the determination in his face. "Which is it going to be, honey?" he pressed.

She swallowed hard. "I'll go with you. Let go of my hair. You're hurting me."

He released his grip, pulled her to her feet, and stepped back. "Get your things together," he said, and a glower on her face, she turned to a heavy suitcase opened across one of the chairs. "Not in that," he growled. "Too damn cumbersome." He saw a linen laundry bag lying nearby and pointed to it.

"My things will get all wrinkled in that," she protested.

"Use it or you'll get all wrinkled," Fargo snapped, thoroughly irritated at her attitude. He'd expected gratitude, not hostility.

She tossed him a glare and began stuffing clothes into the laundry bag. When she finished, she turned to him.

"Now get dressed," he said.

"Not with you watching," she protested.

"I'm not stepping outside, honey," Fargo said. "Dress."

She shrugged, turned her back on him, and stepped to where a shirt and skirt were draped over a chair, a pair of lacy underthings next to them. A small hurricane lamp rested on a small table alongside her things, and he saw her reach for her underthings, lift the garments, and suddenly half-turn, her hand closing around the lamp. She flung it as she whirled, and he ducked as the lamp passed a scant half-inch over his head. His face crinkled into a grimace as the lamp smashed through the window with the loud sound of shattering glass.

"Little bitch," Fargo growled as he swung a short left hook that grazed the point of her lovely chin. But it was enough to send her to the floor unconscious, and he stepped to her, lifted her over one shoulder, and took hold of the laundry bag with the same hand while he yanked the Colt from its holster. He hit the door of the car with his hip as heard the growing murmur of voices outside. He swung from the outside platform of the car, the limp form of the guard still lying there. He dropped to the ground, the young woman bouncing on his shoulder.

A dozen figures were already climbing down from the flatbed car with another three running toward him. Fargo began to run across the ground, as fast as he could with the weight over his shoulder. He wondered how many more seconds he had before someone saw him, and he received the answer just as he finished the thought.

The volley of shots sprayed over his head. He swerved to one side, then the other, and the next volley grazed his shoulder. He flung himself forward and let the young woman roll from his shoulder as he hit the ground. He spun, saw the figures running toward him, three in the forefront, the others a dozen yards behind. The Colt spit flame. The first three pursuers went down, and the others scattered. Fargo was already on his feet, dragging the young woman with him into the mouth of the crevice.

Another fusillade sent chips of stone into the air as the Trailsman paused to lift the girl, fling her across the saddle on her stomach, and pull himself up behind her. He turned the Ovaro around, started up the crevice, and whirled in the saddle as he heard footsteps reach the crevice. He fired the Colt and saw two of the pursuers go down, one atop the other, to block the mouth of the crevice. He urged the Ovaro on up the narrow, twisting passageway, and the shouts below quickly became a distant echo.

They'd be getting horses to follow, but they wouldn't chase him very far from the train, he knew. They couldn't afford to be caught by stray chance on American soil. On the train there was little chance of being stopped and questioned, so they'd be quick to return to the safety of it.

Fargo let the pinto climb the steep and twisting crevice without hurrying, and when he reached the top, he rode across the high rocks at a slow trot.

The rock formation came to an end and he threaded his way down further steep, creviced passages to the flat land below. He heard the girl moan as he put the pinto into a fast trot and she came awake when he turned into a deep hollow of post oak with back ledge of sandstone. He dismounted and helped her slide from the saddle; she swayed for a moment, straightened herself, and let her gray eyes glare at him.

"We bed down here for tonight," he said as he took his lariat from the horse.

"What's that for?" she asked.

"To see that you don't hightail it the minute I fall asleep," Fargo answered. "Unless you want to give me your word you'll stay here."

"I'll take the rope."

"Whatever you say, honey," Fargo remarked, and began to tie her wrists in front of her.

"Don't call me honey," she snapped. "My name is Clare."

He nodded and proceeded to tie her ankles together, then run a length of lariat from her waist to the trunk of a nearby oak, knotting it securely. He returned to where she waited, the cotton nightgown now pulled tighter to reveal the soft swell of what seemed modest breasts.

"I'll get you a blanket," Fargo said.

She stayed tight-lipped as he returned with the bedding and spread it on the ground. She knelt down on it, lowered herself to stretch out, and he watched the pastel loveliness of her shimmer in the moonlight. She had enough slack in the rope to pull the blanket around herself as she watched him undress.

Her eyes stayed on the smoothly muscled symmetry of his body until he was about to pull off the last of his garments. Then she turned on her side, her back to him.

"Good night, Clare, honey," he murmured as he settled down, and he received only silence as a reply.

Fargo lay still and frowned into space for a few minutes. Jill Foster had given him only the barest outline of the task. She knew no more, she had insisted, and perhaps with honesty. But there was more, a lot more, he pondered. Clare Standish's furious hostility was evidence of that. Perhaps she'd decide to be more talkative in the morning. He turned off further thoughts and let sleep wrap itself around him.

The night passed quietly and Fargo woke with the new day, drew on trousers, and watched Clare Standish come awake as the sun brushed its warm rays across her sleeping form. She sat up, her delicate coloring reinforced in the sunlight, every pastel detail heightened. She raised both bound wrists into the air to rub sleep from her eyes with one arm. She blinked, focused on him, and he turned from her to step to the edge of the hollow.

"Aren't you going to untie me?" she protested at once.

"In a minute," he said as he peered toward the now distant high rocks. The land between was empty, no horsemen searching the plains. He turned back to the young woman and untied her bonds. She rose to her feet, her face set tight, and he handed her his canteen.

"Use this to freshen up," he said, and she took it with regal silence, picked up the laundry bag, and stepped behind the nearest oak.

Fargo finished dressing, gave the horse a fast rubdown before Clare reappeared in a pastel-pink shirt and a black riding skirt. He saw long legs, calves nicely shaped, and breasts that seemed as modest as they had under the nightgown.

She halted before him, light gray eyes searching his face. "Who are you?" she asked.

"Name's Skye Fargo. Some call me the Trailsman."

"Where are you taking me?"

"I told you, to your father," Fargo said.

Irritated impatience filled her glance. "Why do you keep lying?"

"Why do you keep disbelieving me?"

"Because *they* were taking me to Herb Standish," Clare flung out.

Fargo knew the frown dug hard into his brow as he stared at the young woman. Thoughts tumbled through his mind in sudden disarray. "Run that past me again," he said.

"The soldiers were taking me to Herb Standish," she repeated impatiently. "So you're lying."

"No," Fargo said, the word falling from his lips and the frown still digging hard at him.

"Why don't you just tell me who sent you to kidnap me?" Clare prodded.

"Herb Standish," Fargo said as thoughts continued to tumble wildly inside his head. Clare's expression was both disdainful and chiding. He let her words run through his mind again. The Mexican soldiers had been taking her to meet Herb Standish, yet he'd been hired to take her from the train. It made no damn sense. "Where were they taking you?"

"They never told me, but I heard them mention a place called Three Rivers."

Fargo's eyes narrowed in thought. His orders were to bring her to Standish in Jonah, a good hundred miles west of Three Rivers. It continued to make no sense, but he had only one hand and he'd have to play it out, he realized. "Let's ride," he muttered, and helped pull her into the saddle.

She turned to look at him. "You going to stick to your stupid story?"

"That's right, honey," he said, and her lips tightened as she turned back and sat stiffly, keeping as much distance from him as she could in the saddle.

Fargo said nothing and Clare grew tired quickly enough. He felt the soft, warm roundness of her rear come back against his thighs. He set a slow pace across the flat land and moved into sandstone formations that rose to his right. A pool with shale surrounding most of it suddenly came into sight. He halted at the edge, where a growth of thick, hard brush formed a line along one side. They had ridden through the morning and he swung from the saddle.

"You want to cool off?" he asked.

"Not with an audience," she said even as she looked longingly at the pool.

"You're putting a strain on my principles," Fargo said.

"Principles?"

"It's against my principles to look away from beauty," he told her.

"Compliments. How unexpected," Clare said, and slid from the saddle. "But it's still no audience."

"Be quick," he grunted. "You'll need a towel."

"I have one in my bag," she said.

Fargo nodded and strode past her to climb up the side of shale. When he reached the top, he swore under his breath as he found that the rock curved upward at the ledge to obscure the pool below.

"Next time," he muttered, and turned his eyes to

the terrain that stretched beyond while he listened to Clare splash in the pool below. No long flat plateaus, he saw, though enough good flat riding land. But it was surrounded by shale and sandstone formations along with stands of short, cone-shaped blackjack oak. He walked along the top of the shale and paused to kneel down to examine a half-dozen short, sun-dried pieces of thin rawhide. Apache boot laces, he grunted, used when the regular laces on captured army boots wore out. He peered out across the terrain and saw nothing move. He rose when the sounds of splashing halted, and he climbed down the shale to the pool and saw Clare behind the brush, arms lifted as she slipped her shirt on.

She stepped into the open while buttoning the top buttons of her shirt and halted at Fargo's question.

"Herb Standish is your father, isn't he?" he asked.

"What made you ask that?" Clare frowned as he fingers buttoned the next button of the shirt.

"Nothing fits right. I wondered if that didn't, too."

"He's my stepfather," Clare answered, her words sheathed in ice.

"And you don't like him," Fargo ventured, and saw her pause in buttoning the shirt, surprise in her eyes as she stared back.

"You pick up quickly," she commented.

"I try," he said laconically.

"You're right, I don't like him. In fact, I hate him," she said with sudden vehemence.

"I was told your mother left him for that Mexican general," Fargo mentioned.

"General Victor de los Santos," Clare said, spitting out the name. "And you were told wrong. She didn't leave Standish. He sold her to the general."

Fargo's eyebrows lifted in surprise. "Sold her?"

"He took us on a trip to Mexico, where he was to meet de los Santos. This was eight years ago. He sold

Mother on the spot to the general. She was his property, he said, and he could do what he wanted with her. With the Mexican attitude toward women, that seemed completely all right. The general was glad to get her. Mother had my coloring then, and she became his prize, a blond Anglo wife. It put a feather in his cap."

Anger and thinking back absorbed Clare's attention, and Fargo saw her fingers move down to close the other buttons on the shirt. But she skipped to the last button in error and left the middle three open.

"Didn't your ma try to escape?" he asked her.

"How and where? She had no money and she was in a strange land. Besides, the general promised her all kinds of things for me, and it was plain she and Herb Standish were through. The general made good on some of them. We had servants and I was sent to schools my mother could never have afforded. So she made her own compromises, most of them for me," Clare said, a sadness coming into her voice. She was still unaware she'd left the three middle buttons of the blouse undone, he saw.

"And now Standish is bringing you back, with the general's help, obviously," Fargo said. "Why?"

Her eyes studied him for a long moment. "I don't know," she said, and he smiled inwardly. She knew more than what she was saying, but she didn't trust him enough for the truth. His eyes passed over the open buttons of the blouse where he glimpsed the softly curved edge of one breast. "Who sent you for me?" she asked.

"We've gone over that," he said, and her lips thinned with instant anger, stubbornness coming into her face.

"Then don't bother to ask me any more questions about anything. You won't get any answers," she said angrily.

"Wouldn't think of it," he said blandly. "But I am curious about one thing."

"What's that?" She frowned.

"Why you left the three middle buttons of your shirt open," he said mildly.

A swallowed yelp escaped her lips as she looked down at the shirt and clapped one hand to the unbuttoned gap. She pulled buttons closed instantly, and her cheeks were flushed when she finished and looked back at him.

"Didn't see much," he said.

"Not because you didn't try," she accused.

"Maybe because there's not much to see." He pulled back as her hand grazed his cheek.

"You go to hell," she hissed.

He smiled at her. "Maybe later. Right now we ride."

3

Clare rode in angry silence that finally simmered down as the day wore on. Fargo continued to pause to peer at the trails of unshod pony prints that crossed their path. "Indians?" she questioned finally.

"Apache," Fargo grunted. "Nothing fresh enough to worry about yet. Not that that's a lot of reassurance. This is all Apache country, and that means you can expect anything anytime."

"They're very fierce?" Clare asked.

"That's as good a word as any. More important, the Apache and the land are one. They use the land differently than any other Indian: they have their own ways of fighting and that's been the death of many a horse patrol used to the ways of the Plains Indians," he told her.

"Have you ever fought the Apache?" Clare asked.

"Fought them, dealt with them, played wits with them."

"You're still alive."

"It's a small club," Fargo grunted grimly.

Clare regarded him with a long long. "You're obviously very good at what you do."

"Admiration?" He laughed. "That's a step in the right direction."

"Observation," she sniffed. "I can admire the skill with which a rattler strikes without admiring the rattler."

"One for you," he said, and spurred the pinto forward.

The land dipped, rose, dipped again, and the day was nearing an end when the Trailsman spotted the collection of antelope jackrabbits bounding among the low rocks. He drew the big Sharps from its rifle case alongside the saddle, surveyed the distant terrain again, and decided to risk the sound. He swung to the ground, moved to a low rock, took aim on one of the long-eared targets, paused, and decided to wait for a better shot. He wanted only one shot to resound across the land.

Suddenly one of the rangy, long-eared, long-legged forms bounded into his sights. Fargo fired and the jackrabbit twisted in midair before falling to the ground. He hurried to the animal, scooped it up, and led the Ovaro on to where he spotted a small inset of rock and tall, tangly shrub. "We make camp here," he said, and Clare slid to the ground.

"I don't know how to skin a rabbit," she said.

"I'll take care of that. You round up a couple dozen stones, more or less the same size," he said.

"I don't have to do this," Clare said stiffly, not moving.

"You don't have to eat, either," Fargo said.

She let another moment pass but then turned and began to search the ground.

The Trailsman took the thin, sharp, double-edged throwing knife from the calf holster around his leg and began to skin the big jackrabbit. He was finished when she returned with a second load of stones and dumped them on the ground. "I'll show you an Apache trail fire," he said, and began to form a circle of the stones. He piled a second layer atop the first, then a third, and soon the circle of stones stood a little over two feet high. "Get some small pieces of wood and brush, lots of brush for a hot fire," he ordered.

She hurried to obey this time with no snide remarks.

He had the fire going soon, blazing at the bottom of the circle of stones, and he made a makeshift spit for the hare and laid the animal across the top of the stones over the fire. The stones grew hot quickly and the hare began to roast at once.

"Plenty of heat to stay warm by, plenty of flame for roasting, and no fire's glow to be seen from a distance," he said as he stretched out near the circle of stones.

Clare sat down nearby, arms folded across her knees. There was enough soft glow rising from the circle of stones to give her pastel coloring a shimmering beauty.

"You ever see a spotted jewelweed?" he asked.

"No," she answered.

"It's a flower of delicate beauty that hangs from its long stem as though it were a dainty earring that might fall off at the slightest touch. But it doesn't, and its stem is tough and strong. I think you're like a spotted jewelweed," he said.

Her smile was slow. "Admiration?" She laughed. "That's a step in the right direction."

"Observation," he said. "Lots of dangerous things fool you by being beautiful on the outside."

"One for you. That makes us even," she said.

Fargo chuckled with her and took the roasted hare from over the fire and used the slender throwing knife to cut pieces off for Clare and himself.

"I didn't realize how hungry I was," she said between bites, and when they finished, there was enough meat left over to set aside and let dry out. She rose, took her nightgown from the canvas bag, and stepped behind the brush and he had the blanket and his bedroll out when she returned.

He flicked a glance to the lariat hanging from the strap on the form swell of the saddle. "Your choice," he said.

"I'm going to take any chance I get to run away from you," Clare said firmly.

He shrugged and took the lariat down. "Then I've no choice."

"I might feel differently if you told me why you took me from the train and what this is all about," she offered.

He paused for a moment and let her words hang in his mind. "I'd like to know that myself, Clare, honey," he said.

The wryness of his answer was lost on her as she glared at him while he tied her thoroughly, this time fastening the long length of line around a thin rock.

He stepped to his bedroll and began to undress, aware that she watched him though she pretended to stare into the night. He paused as he reached his underdrawers. "You going to turn away again tonight?" he remarked into the night, heard her sharp intake of breath and then the sound of her turning her back on him.

"I wasn't watching," she muttered.

"Didn't your mother tell you it's not nice to lie?" He chuckled, and silence was his only reply. He settled onto his bedroll and fell asleep quickly, waking only once as Clare noisily turned on the blanket.

When morning came, he hurried her into waking and rode west while the sun was still easing down the high rocks. The day grew burning hot, the dry land a mirror that reflected the sun's rays. He halted twice during the morning to rest the horse: the first time beside a trickle of a stream where he filled his canteen and Clare cooled her wrists in the water; the second at a stand of elderberries that provided a sweet lunch.

As the day wore on, he saw that Clare's shirt had grown damp with perspiration and clung to her, outlining the curve of her breasts, the cups turning upward, the faintest indication of tiny points touching the material.

By late afternoon the terrain had turned mountainous, mostly granite and sandstone. There was still enough black oak to afford some shade and moisture from the sun's relentless rays. He had moved up along a trail through granite outcroppings when he reined to a sharp halt.

"Get down," he hissed as he swung to the ground and led the Ovaro into a niche in the granite. He motioned for Clare to stay close behind him as he moved on foot through a crevice passageway in the rock.

"Apache?" she asked, fear in her voice.

"No."

"How can you be so sure?" she asked with a trace of impatience.

"I heard the sound of rein chains. Apaches don't use rein chains or bits," he murmured. He halted at the top of the passage to peer out at a path that crossed from left to right through the rocks. He stayed, hardly breathing, and the horsemen appeared in a few moments—five, he counted, three in front, two following.

"They're white men," Clare breathed.

"Bandits," Fargo grunted as he took in the extra cartridge belts across their chests and the empty sacks folded behind their saddles. "They hole up in these hills."

He saw Clare frown at him. "You don't know that," she said.

"I know," he growled. "Stay down and stay quiet." His gaze was on the riders who slowly crossed in front of him when the blow struck his shoulder, knocked him half-forward, and he looked up to see Clare's form leaping past him into the open. He grabbed for her, managed a half-grip on one leg as she pulled away.

"Here, over here," she was shouting as she half-dived, half-fell onto the trail. "Help me. I'm being held prisoner."

Fargo saw the riders spin their horses in surprise, drawing six-guns automatically and watching as Clare stumbled toward them.

"He's behind those rocks. He kidnapped me," she cried out.

The lead rider, a man with a long jaw and narrow eyes, watched her for a moment, and Fargo saw the delight flare in the narrow eyes. "Blast him," the man shouted, and Fargo ducked as the fusillade slammed into the rocks. They hadn't seen him, but they were spray-shooting to keep him in place.

"Damn little bitch," Fargo swore as he dived down the crevice, slipping, skidding headfirst on a smooth stretch of rock. He barely managed to avoid bashing his head in. He rose, started to race for the Ovaro, and reached the horse just as two of the men climbed over the rocks, guns drawn. He crouched, started to pull the Colt when he saw two more climb over the rocks at his back. "Damn," he muttered as he let the Colt drop back into the holster. They had him out-flanked and they were too close for all of them to miss. He straightened, led the Ovaro from the niche, and faced the four men.

"This way, mister," one said, and gestured to a break in the rocks. Fargo led the Ovaro with him and stepped onto the passage to see Clare beside the one with the long jaw and narrow eyes. The man watched him approach, an oily grin sliding across his face. Greasy black hair covered his head and a gold chain hung over the two crossed cartridge belts he wore.

"So you kidnapped this beautiful little girl, did you, mister?" the man said. "Now, what'd you figure to do with her all by yourself?"

Fargo halted, his eyes ice-floe blue as they bored

into the man, flicked to Clare for an instant, and saw the triumph in her face. He returned his gaze to the bandit leader. "None of your damn business," the Trailsman said, and saw the narrow eyes grow narrower.

"Smart ass, are you?" the man growled. "Get his gun." Fargo stood quietly as one of the others lifted the Colt from his holster. The man turned to Clare. "Get on his horse, girlie. He can walk. We're going down out of these rocks."

"If you get me to Three Rivers you'll be well-paid," Clare said.

The man smiled at her. "Jimmy. The name's Jimmy," he said.

"All right, Jimmy." Clare smiled back. "Just get me to Three Rivers."

"She wasn't going to Three Rivers," Fargo cut in. "She's lying to you."

Jimmy turned his gaze back to Clare. "A little beauty like this lie? I don't believe it," he said, and Fargo's eyes swept the other four as they laughed. One wore a paunch that his cartridge belts barely managed to circle. Two others were small-faced, sallow-complexioned, and the fifth one a thin, bony character with a gaunt face and straggly black beard—all soulless, heartless, small-time killers, outcasts even among outcasts.

But for now Fargo could only buy time. He watched as the leader walked Clare to the Ovaro, stood close to the horse as she started to pull herself into the saddle. She was halfway up in the stirrup when the man's hand shot under the riding skirt, and Clare screamed as she vaulted onto the horse. She turned, her lips parted, and frowned down at Jimmy's grinning face.

"Don't you ever do that again," she snapped.

"Honey, you belong to us now. We'll do whatever we want with you. We saved you from that kidnapper, remember?" The man broke into a high-pitched laughter. He kept hold of the Ovaro's reins as he climbed onto his own horse and gestured to Fargo. "Keep an eye on him, Bones," he ordered, and the gaunt-faced man swung in at the rear as the others started downhill.

"Where are we going?" Clare asked the leader.

"Away from these rocks and down to some grassland," Jimmy said.

"That's right," one of the sallow-faced pair agreed. "We don't want your little ass bouncin' on rock when we give it to you."

A guffaw rose from the others, and Fargo, walking alongside the Ovaro, saw the comprehension begin to dawn in Clare's face as, her mouth open, she stared at the five men.

"Happy?" he murmured, unable to resist the moment.

She looked at him, her eyes filled with shocked horror as the full realization swept over her. He almost felt sorry for her, but he reminded himself, she'd put his neck in a noose, too. She continued to stare at him, speechless, totally overwhelmed by the monstrousness of her error. She finally pulled her eyes away to stare down at her hands as she held the saddle horn.

Fargo saw the grayness of dusk sliding over the rocks and Jimmy found a level place with a carpet of drop-seed grass and a good stand of condelia.

"This'll do right fine," the man said, and tied the Ovaro to a low branch as the others dismounted. He reached up and pulled Clare from the saddle, one hand clasping her rear. She spun, aimed a blow at his face, and he ducked away, his grin disappearing. He slammed a fist into her side and she fell with a gasp of pain as the other four gathered around her. "That's enough of that shit, girlie," Jimmy rasped, and yanked her to her feet.

"Let's get rid of him first," the gaunt-faced one said, and nodded to Fargo.

"Yeah, we don't need an audience," Jimmy said.

"I'll make you a deal," Fargo said quickly. He'd formed the offer on the walk down, the only one he could devise that might appeal to the scurvy lot.

"Deal? You can't make a deal on anything, mister," Jimmy sneered. "You're vulture bait."

"I didn't think you boys were the kind to turn away from three hundred dollars," Fargo said mildly, and saw the man's brows lift at once.

"You got three hundred dollars?" Jimmy asked.

"I will tomorrow morning," Fargo said.

"That's a lot of money, mister. Talk," the bandit leader said.

"A man's meeting me in the morning, not far from where you jumped me," Fargo said. "He's to pay me three hundred dollars for her." He glanced at Clare for an instant and returned his eyes to Jimmy. "He buys girls, takes them across the border. He doesn't pay that usually, but for someone like her, with her looks and untouched, he agreed to three hundred."

The five men exchanged quick glances and Jimmy let his lips purse in thought. "What's the deal, mister?"

"I take you to him, come morning. You sell her to him, take the three hundred, and I walk away," Fargo said. "But he won't buy unless she's fresh and untouched as she is now." He lapsed into silence and waited, watching the men exchange quick glances again. He could almost follow the wheels as they turned in Jimmy's mind. He'd given them a choice they couldn't turn down, a situation practically tailored to their way of thinking. They'd bring Clare to the place, take the three hundred, kill the buyer, and they'd still have her to enjoy for themselves. Of course, they'd kill him, too, as soon as the buy was finished, he realized. But buying the night was all that mattered now. He waited, watched Jimmy review everything once more in his mind and finally nod.

"All right, mister, you got yourself a deal," the bandit leader agreed.

Fargo congratulated himself with silent wryness on having read the man's character with such grim accuracy. He snapped a glance at Clare, who'd had the sense to stay quiet, though he saw the bewilderment in her eyes.

"Tie them both up," Jimmy ordered, and two of the others approached Fargo and Clare at once.

Fargo held his arms out in front of him obediently and the gaunt-faced man began to bind his wrists together. These were really small-time, stupid killers. Fargo began to feel more confident about his plans. He was taken to the nearest condelia; his ankles were bound and then he was strapped to the tree. They did the same with Clare and sat her alongside him as night descended. They made a small fire and cooked beans and beef jerky as Clare's whispered questions drifted to him.

"Why'd you tell them that story? What good is it going to do? They'll know it was all a lie, come morning," she said.

"The hell with morning. I needed the night to try to get us out of here," Fargo muttered. He followed with an oath as he saw Jimmy produce a bottle of whiskey from his saddlebag.

"Maybe it'll be better if they drink themselves into a stupor," Clare suggested.

"No," Fargo hissed. "They'll be drinking halfway through the night now, and that won't leave me enough time." He swore again as he watched the men began to pass the bottle among one another.

The Trailsman let an hour go by and shook his head in frustration. They were drinking slowly, regaling one another with stories of women and shoot-outs, all thoroughly embroidered, he was certain. But the fire had become only embers and the condelia where they were tied was in blackness. He couldn't risk waiting any longer, he decided. He would need every moment.

Moving both bound wrists together, Fargo reached his arms downward, hooked the fingers of one hand under the cuff of his trousers, and began to pull the pants leg up. Letting his fingers move crablike, he inched the cuff upward, pulling both arms along, until he passed the smooth leather of the calf holster and finally managed to rest his fingers upon the hilt of the slender, double-edged throwing knife. Gripping the hilt between the end of his forefinger and thumb, he carefully drew the blade from its holster and let his trouser cuff drop down to his ankle again. He drew a deep sigh, but he had the knife out, albeit in a precarious grip. He looked across at the five men and saw they hadn't moved except to change position as they continued to talk and drink.

Fargo carefully turned the thin blade in his fingers, drew both wrists up, and turned the blade again so that the point faced him. Using only the ends of his fingers in the only grip he could get on the knife, he began to move the blade back and forth against the wrist ropes, each sawing motion not more than a quarter of an inch long.

The Trailsman quickly found that though the knife was razor-sharp, the constricted sawing motion made only a shallow cut each time, his position too cramped to exert any weight on the blade. He also found that he had to halt every few minutes when his fingers cramped. Cutting into the wrist ropes became an agonizingly painful and slow task. Each time he had to stop he looked across the darkness at the bandits. He had just halted again to let the ends of his fingers unstiffen when he saw the bandits had stopped drinking.

Jimmy rose to his feet and returned the half-empty bottle to his saddlebag. "Enough," the bandit leader said. "We don't want any fuzzed-up heads, come morning." He dragged a blanket from his gear and settled down on it. "Bones, go check on our friends," he said.

"Damn," Fargo murmured, and let the slender knife fall from his fingers. It landed on the ground directly in front of him, and he managed to move enough to cover it with his left leg. He kept his bound wrists stretched out in front of him as the gaunt-faced man approached and squinted down at him, then cast a longer glance at Clare. Satisfied that everything was in order, Bones walked back to the others.

Fargo heard Clare's heartfelt sigh of relief. He sat silently and watched the bandits settle down to sleep, and only when he heard their snores and steady, heavy breathing did he move his leg from the knife. He brought both hands down to the ground again, still bound together, groped for the knife, and finally closed his fingers around the hilt. He slowly brought both arms up, the knife held in his fingers, and once more carefully turned the blade around so he could begin to saw at the wrist ropes again.

The task grew harder as he went along, his fingers cramping more frequently while the rests in between grew longer. But suddenly he felt the ropes around his wrists loosen, then come apart, and he dropped his hands into his lap, rested for another moment, and then pulled the ropes free. He massaged circulation back into his wrists and then, able to bring pressure now, cut the ropes around his ankles with one, quick, slicing blow. The rope binding his body to the tree came next and he snapped it open and turned to Clare. "I'm going to cut you loose," he said. "But you don't move. Stay exactly as you are and leave the ropes in place."

She nodded and he quickly cut the ropes that bound her, reached around, and severed the rope that bound her to the tree at the rear of the trunk.

Finished, Fargo moved back to his position against

49

the condelia, placed the body ropes under his armpits so they seemed taut cross his chest, then wrapped his ankles and wrists tight enough for the ropes to hold in place and appear still tied. He allowed a deep sigh to escape him as he relaxed against the tree trunk.

"We just going to stay here like this?" Clare asked, protest in her voice.

"That's right," he said.

"We're free. Why don't we just crawl away?"

"This is dry-ground grass. It rustles like taffeta. I don't know that I could crawl across it quietly, and I know you sure as hell won't without waking them. We're finished, then. We won't get another chance," Fargo said. "Besides, I'll need a gun to give us any chance. That means we have to bring one of them over to us."

"We just sit here till morning?" Clare said.

"No. You catnap, doze, get some sleep. That's what I'm going to do. And don't move. Everything has to look right in the morning," Fargo said. Sliding the slender knife against his forearm, he let the hilt of the blade rest in his palm, put his head back, and quickly slept.

Morning came some three hours later. Fargo woke with the first rays of the sun, glanced at Clare, and saw her pull her eyes open.

The men stirred, slowly pulled themselves awake, the bandit leader the first to get to his feet, the gaunt-faced man next.

"Check on them, Bones," Jimmy ordered as the other three slowly began to get up.

Fargo's lips hardly moved as he slid words at Clare.

"The minute I make my move, you dive for cover, throw yourself to the back of the tree, understand?" he said, and she nodded. His eyes were on the man who approached. They were merciless killers, the lot of them, he reminded himself. They intended to kill him when the time came, and Clare when they'd had enough of her. He slid the double-edged blade from beside his forearm, the hilt still firmly against his palm.

Bones halted in front of him, stared down at him.

Fargo raised both wrists, which appeared still bound. "They're cutting my skin. They're too tight," he said.

Bones leaned down for a closer look and Fargo flipped the knife in the palm of his hand, ripped the blade upward and forward from the man's abdomen into his solar plexus. The gaunt face seemed to grow thinner as the man's mouth fell open in shock and pain and his eyes widened in surprise for an instant before he toppled forward.

Fargo rolled out of the way and yanked the man's gun from its holster as he did. He spun, glimpsed Clare diving for the other side of the tree as the other four men turned toward him. He fired at once; the two sallow-faced men went down in a tangle of arms and legs. He rolled, flung himself into the tangly brush as the volley of return fire slammed into the ground where he had been.

The Trailsman started to fire off another shot and held back. Jimmy had already reached the cover of a condelia and the fifth man had disappeared into a niche in a tall rock. He shot a glance at Clare, who lay facedown behind the tree. "Stay there," he ordered, sliding back deeper into the brush. Suddenly he leapt to his feet. But his eyes were on the condelia opposite him, and he saw Jimmy half-rise, fire a hasty volley of shots, and sink down behind the tree again as he saw his target duck down. But Fargo had the spot where the man waited marked in his mind now. "Clare," he called in a whisper, and the girl's head lifted. "Get up enough to make a flying dive to your right."

Clare nodded, rose to a half-crouch, and Fargo's gun was leveled at the spot where the bandit leader had come up to fire. She gathered herself, rose, and dived forward, the sound loud in the tense silence.

Jimmy half-rose again to fire, his form moving into Fargo's already sighted aim, and the Trailsman pressed the trigger, a single shot, and the bandit leader's forehead erupted in a spray of red and his figure flew backward.

Fargo didn't move as he heard the man's body thud into the ground. Then, slowly, he brought the gun to the niche in the rock. The pistol, a Joslyn army revolver, had only a five-shot chamber, and that left him with but one remaining bullet. The heavy man with the paunch had kept absolutely silent in the niche, but he had a partial view of the open space outside. He had seen at least two of his partners fall.

Fargo motioned for Clare to come to him. "Work your way to the horses. Ride the Ovaro and pull one of the others with you. Take off along the side where he can't see you from the niche," he said.

Fargo waited a moment to let her get a start and then called out. "Come out with your hands up and you can walk away," he said.

"Go to hell," the answer came.

"You're trapped in there. Get smart," Fargo said.

"Come in and get me," the man returned.

"Sure, you'd like that, wouldn't you?" Fargo answered. "You can't get out. I'm offering you your life."

"Shove it," the man rasped.

Fargo smiled. Fatso had his own scurvy wiliness. He was counting on two things: one, that his former captives would decide to light out instead of playing the waiting game, and two, that he'd wait till nightfall if necessary and then slip from the niche. Fargo brought his eyes to the horses and saw Clare pulling herself onto the Ovaro. The paunchy one was about to have one of his calculations take form. Clare looked toward him from atop the Ovaro as she took the reins of one of the other horses in hand. He raised his arm and brought in forward in a short, fast motion, and Clare sent the Ovaro dashing forward, hoofbeats an instant tattoo on the dry soil.

Fargo had the gun raised as the paunchy figure ran from the niche and brought his gun up to fire at Clare. Fargo's last shot exploded first and the side of the man's head seemed to vanish as he slammed sideways into the rock and slid to the ground, a grotesque shape with but half a head and a paunch splattered with red.

Clare looked back and reined to a halt as she saw Fargo step into the clear. She turned and rode back toward him as he retrieved his Colt from the bandit leader's belt and then the thin-bladed knife, which he wiped clean on the grass. She halted, slid to the ground, and her gray eyes were filled with both shock and relief as she scanned the scene.

"Let's get out of here," Fargo said, and swung onto the Ovaro. "You ride the other horse."

She nodded and followed as he set a fast pace away from the trees. They rode into the high land again and continued on until the terrain grew less harsh with long stands of black oak among the rock formations.

It was past noon when he spotted a stream. He drew to a halt and watched Clare dismount, sit down at the edge of the stream, and wash the cool water over her face and arms. He had knelt beside her and refilled his canteen when he saw her body trembling uncontrollably. He reached toward her; she came against him at once and he felt the softness of her breasts as she clung to him.

"It all just swept over me again," she murmured. "I'm sorry," she said as the trembling came to a stop and she pulled back. There were no tears, he noted, only the remains of shock in the light gray eyes. "Thank you for saving us, for saving me," she said. "I don't blame you for being angry with me."

"That's nice," he muttered.

"Tell me where you're taking me! Tell me who sent you to do this," she cried.

"I've told you that," he said, and saw disappointment mix with the instant anger in her face.

"Then I'll try to get away again. I have to," she said with sudden desperation.

"Try to be smarter about it next time," he said, and she managed a rueful half-smile.

"I'll try," she murmured. "You make it difficult."

"How?" he asked.

"It's hard to be grateful and angry at the same time," she said.

"I'm sure you'll manage," he said with a grin. "Let's ride."

4

Fargo rode hard and Clare stayed with him without complaint, and when night came, he found a place to camp beside a tall, broad-branched pecan. They finished the meat of the hare that he had saved, and the moon rose to add a patina of silver to Clare's pastel beauty.

"Jewelweed," Fargo grunted as she stretched out on both elbows, breasts turned upward under the shirt.

"I'll take that as a compliment," she said.

"Time to get some sleep," he said, and let his eyes ask the question.

"I promise," she said. "But only for the night."

"All right," Fargo agreed. "But you break that promise and you'll wish you hadn't."

"I promised," Clare said reproachfully, and she took her things and disappeared around the tree. He had his bedroll down and her blanket out when she returned, lost again in the folds of the nightgown. She lay down at once, but this time she turned her back on him the minute he began to undress.

"No watching tonight?" he remarked, and received no answer. "I'm wondering what that means."

"It means I'm a proper lady," she said, not turning.

"Or one afraid of herself," Fargo said, and again had only silence as an answer. He smiled as he closed his eyes and let sleep sweep him away. When morning came, he again set a hard pace, stopping only to breakfast on a stand of wild plums. It was just past the noon hour when a town came into sight.

"Jonah," he said, and congratulated himself on finding the place on the first try. He saw the apprehension cross Clare's face at once as she rode beside him to the town.

Jonah was a place that hardly deserved to be called a town, a half-dozen buildings, one a saloon, one a stable, and one a boardinghouse, the other three ramshackle structures that were as much falling down as standing up.

Fargo silently cursed the lack of any detailed instructions from Jill Foster and decided on the boardinghouse as the most likely place to start. He took Clare inside with him and saw a man in a tan shirt and tan stetson leaning near the front desk. The clerk, an elderly man with a cane, hobbled to the desk. "Name's Fargo," the Trailsman said. "Any messages for me?"

The clerk started to shake his head when the man in the tan shirt straightened up.

"Been waiting on you all week," he said.

"I'm here. Be satisfied with that," Fargo said.

"Lew Barkins," the man said. "Come with me."

Fargo nodded and followed the man out of the boardinghouse. He held Clare's arm and saw the nervousness in her face.

Riding a short-legged quarter horse, Lew Barkins led the way from town, turned west, climbed a rock-strewn hillside, and when it leveled off, they rode to where an oversized log cabin and a bunkhouse took up most of a cleared parcel of land. Fargo noted four horses tethered nearby and he dismounted as Lew Barkins halted in front of the cabin. He motioned to Clare and she slid to the ground just as the man strode from the house. Fargo, his eyes on Clare, felt the furrow dig into his brow as he saw the astonishment flood her face.

"My God, it *is* you," she breathed as the man halted in front of her.

"In person," the man said, his eyes devouring the girl. "My, you've grown into something special, haven't you?" he said. He turned his eyes to Fargo for a moment. "Herb Standish," he said. "You're Fargo, of course."

Fargo nodded and took in Herb Standish, a man of medium height, trim enough, with a receding forehead and brown hair, a square face with a thrusting jaw, a short nose, and smallish eyes. Standish had a shrewd and crafty face, but Fargo found none of the ruthless strength in it that Jill Foster had described.

"Congratulations, Fargo," Standish said. "You pulled it off. You're everything I heard you were."

"I had questions then. I've more now," Fargo said.

"We can talk inside," Standish said. "I rented this place for a few weeks only. I expect to be moving on in a matter of days."

Fargo, Clare beside him, followed Standish into a cabin that had been divided into a main room and two smaller ones. He felt Clare tug at his elbow.

"I owe you an apology," she said, gray eyes round. "You were telling the truth all along. No wonder you couldn't understand it. I don't either."

"I aim to find out," Fargo growled.

"You can have that room at the right, Clare," Standish said. "It's real good to see you again, my dear."

"I hope you don't expect me to echo those sentiments," Clare answered coldly.

Standish let an oily smile cross his face and glanced at Fargo. "She's turned out very much like her mother, not nearly as delicate as she appears to be."

"I noticed," Fargo said.

"Now, you had some questions, Fargo." Standish smiled.

"Clare told me the Mexican soldiers were bringing

her to you. Why'd you have me steal her off the train, then?" Fargo asked.

Standish's smile grew benevolently tolerant and Fargo again decided the man was clever and crafty, yet evidence of the ruthless strength still escaped him.

"An understandable question. General de los Santos and I had an agreement—a pact, if you will. Our roles and positions were clearly outlined. At the last minute, the general decided to change some of the things in our agreement. Taking Clare from his men was my way of making him realize he had to observe our original agreement," Standish explained. "By now his men have returned to tell him that Clare is completely in my hands. I also sent a messenger to him. I expect our original agreement, in its proper form, will be in my hands in a few days. The general understands the meaning of power."

"What makes Clare so important in all this?" Fargo said, and glanced at the young woman.

She met his glance for a moment and quickly looked away.

"That's a private matter, I'm afraid," Herb Standish said.

"What's this pact between you and the general?" Fargo asked.

"That's not your concern, either," Standish said, retaining his tolerant smile.

"Two thousand dollars still due me is my concern," Fargo growled.

"Indeed it is, but that's not due you until you've finished the job," Standish said.

"I just finished it. She's here, delivered," Fargo said, and looked at Clare again.

She continued to look away.

"No, no, Fargo. It's finished when you guide us safely to the Uvalde Flats country," Standish corrected.

"I was told the balance was due on my delivering the girl," Fargo insisted. "That's what Jill Foster said."

Standish let himself look almost apologetic. "Then she told you wrong. Or she misunderstood my instructions. The balance of the money will be yours the minute you get us to Uvalde Flats."

"Where's Jill Foster?" Fargo questioned.

"She's gone. She left as soon as she reported back to me. There was no reason for her to stay here any longer," the man said.

Fargo paused, searching for words, afraid that if he exposed Standish's methods the man might take his anger out on Clare. The entire relationship was draped in shadows he hadn't pierced yet. "I take it you settled up properly with Jill," he said, certain Standish would understand the unsaid.

"Absolutely," Standish said, unbothered by the question.

Fargo swore silently. He felt like walking away, but that would be stupidity. He was owed two thousand dollars, and walking away wasn't going to get him the money. He was stuck, whether by design or misunderstanding.

Herb Standish's voice snapped off his thoughts. "Can we count on your services, Fargo? You've done so magnificently up to now."

"Doesn't look as though I've much choice," Fargo muttered.

"I knew you'd make the logical decision," Standish said with oily triumph. "There's a cot in the bunkhouse for you."

"I might stay off in the hills," Fargo said.

"I've a better idea. As I have to wait for the general's courier, why don't you go to town tomorrow for a few days rest and relaxation?" Standish said.

"In Jonah?" Fargo frowned.

"I was thinking of Wellsville. It's a half-day's ride, but it's a proper town, been made into a real community. It's the last settled place on the Oxbow Trail before going on to California. It's also the end of the Butterfield overland mail route."

"I might just do that." Fargo nodded. As he turned to leave he cast another glance at Clare. She continued to stare away and he half-shrugged and strode from the large cabin. He had reached the Ovaro when he heard the footsteps running after him.

"Fargo," she called, and he halted, waited for her to reach him. "I didn't know who really sent you. I couldn't talk to you. Can you understand that?"

"I guess so," he said. "But it's different now."

"Yes, but I have to find a time and place. There are things I can't talk about yet," she said. "Meanwhile, I'll be perfectly safe for now. I didn't want you to worry about me."

"What made you think I would?" he slid back, and saw hurt flash in her eyes before anger pushed it aside.

"I apologize. I'd no business assuming that," she said stiffly, and spun on her heel.

He caught her arm and turned her to him again. "Sorry," he said. "That wasn't fair of me. I'd have worried some."

She glared for a moment, but the glare faded away and her gray eyes grew soft. She smiled, a sudden, childlike happiness in it, as though someone worrying over her was a new experience. "Thank you," she murmured, and hurried away.

He watched her disappear into the cabin and went on to the bunkhouse, where four men lounged on their bunks, two empty bunks to one side. One was the man with the tan shirt.

"So you're the Trailsman," Lew Barkins said as Fargo put his things on one of the empty bunks. "Heard about you when I was riding trail up Montana Territory."

"What'd you hear?" Fargo inquired.

"That you're real good," the man said.

"I try." Fargo laughed. "Any of you know what all this is about?"

"No. We were hired as bodyguards for Standish, and that's all we know," Barkins said. "But it's plain he's got big plans about something."

"You curious?" Fargo asked.

"I learned being curious can get a man in trouble," one of the others answered.

"It can," Fargo agreed, and he finished setting his things out.

Night came quickly and he welcomed sleep. When the new day arrived, he saddled up without hurrying. Two of the four men had stayed the night in front of the oversize cabin, he saw as they returned to the bunkhouse. Lew Barkins and the fourth man took up positions outside the house for the morning.

Fargo was ready to ride when Clare came from the house, lemon-blond hair shimmering in the new sun. "You and Stepdaddy have a nice evening talking about old times?" he asked.

"Hardly. He knows I detest him. Most of his questions were about the general." She waited till he finished tightening the cinch, and her gray eyes searched his face when he straightened up. "You're not going to decide to just keep on riding, are you?" she asked.

"That's suddenly important to you?" Fargo asked.

"Yes," she said. "Surprised?"

"Some."

"There are a lot of things. I still can't talk about them now."

"I'll be back," he told her.

Her eyes narrowed as she gave him a searching inspection. "I'm wondering if you'd come back just because I asked you, if the two thousand dollars wasn't part of it," she said.

"Guess you'll have to keep wondering about that, Clare, honey." Fargo smiled and pulled himself into the saddle. He reached down and gave her a pat on the cheek and sent the Ovaro into a fast trot. He rode due west, as Lew Barkins had said to do, letting the Ovaro set his own leisurely pace while the sun burned hot.

When the sun crossed the noon hour, the Trailsman halted in the shade of a tall slab of granite. He rested until the midafternoon shadows began to slide in their sideways fashion across the land. He took to the saddle again, saw a line of unshod Indian pony prints, and turned away in a wide circle.

But he reached Wellsville with the daylight still on the land. He passed a dozen ranches and small farms just outside town and took in the shape of a settled community.

Wellsville itself turned out to be a proper town with a bank, a meeting hall, and a church as well as the usual dance hall. He saw well-dressed ladies on the streets. At one side of town, there were long rows of Conestoga wagons and ox-drawn Owensboro mountain wagons and men in traveling clothes and women in work dresses. Wellsville, he decided, had made itself into a last outpost of civilized living before the terrible trail into California, a living memory the pioneers could take with them to cling to during the dark times.

Fargo drew up in front of a painted house that called itself an inn, took a neat, well-tended room from a young man at the front desk, washed and changed his shirt, and returned to the streets outside. Dusk was sliding into night as he left the pinto outside the inn and strolled through the town. He paused at the dance hall for a sandwich of buffalo strips cooked rare, added a bourbon, and then returned to stroll on along the main street. He slowed as he passed a building with a sign hung over the front door. CORBY'S TRAVELING THEATER, he read, and his eyes moved down to the sandwich sign placed alongside the door.

T O N I G H T
ABBY'S STORY
by
Will Beatty

Starring
Everybody's Favorite
Actress
JILL FOSTER

Fargo started to go on when his head snapped back, his eyes riveting on the last name. "Jill Foster," he murmured aloud. "Actress. By God, actress!" He felt the anger spiraling inside himself, all mixed with disbelief or, he realized, the stronger feeling, the unwillingness to believe. But the sign held his gaze as if it were a magnet. "Actress," he breathed again. "Damn," he half-shouted, and wrested his eyes from the sign. The certainty crystallized inside him, then the rage, first at having been played for a fool, second at having let himself be a party to it.

As he stood before the sign, a man and woman brushed past him, tickets in hand, and entered the theater. Another couple followed, then an elderly pair of women, everyone dressed in their finery, and he saw others disembarking from carriages that drew up in front of the small theater. He spun on his heel, trotted to the narrow alleyway at the side of the building, and saw the side door halfway down the passage. He was at it in three long strides, pulled it open, and slipped inside the building. He found himself in the dim recesses of the theater and across from him, the stage, brightly lighted, and the curtain down.

The set was a mock living room, a sofa in the center, two small tables at the sides, and a backdrop of fake walls. A narrow corridor led from one end of the stage to the back of the theater, and he hurried down it on silent steps to where a partly open door emitted a stream of light. He halted at the door, peered in, and saw a small dressing room, a mirror and makeup table, and Jill Foster seated at it applying rouge to her cheeks.

She was stunning in a bare-shouldered black evening gown, he saw with a stab of bitterness. He pushed the door all the way open and slammed it behind him as he stepped into the room.

Jill turned around on the narrow bench, her eyes widening in astonishment. "Fargo," she gasped.

"Himself," he said. "Came by to see that great actress, Miss Jill Foster."

He saw the instant caution come into her eyes, but she put forth a bright smile. "What a wonderful surprise. Then you're going to stay and see the play," she said.

He smiled back. " 'Fraid not. You see, I've already seen her in one of her greatest performances."

Jill swallowed as she rose to her feet, and he saw the moment of alarm flash in her eyes. "Now, wait, Fargo. We can talk about it after the play. The curtain's going up in five minutes," she said. "I'll explain everything then." She tried the bright smile again, but it disappeared as his hand shot out, closed over the neckline of the gown, and pulled her forward.

"There never was any little sister, was there?" he rasped. "You made her up to get me to go along with you."

"I had a lot of debts to pay off. I needed the money Standish promised me," she said.

"So you got me to risk my neck and put me into God knows what. You gave me a cock-and-bull story. You lied and laid your way through all of it," Fargo thundered.

"I'm sorry," she said, and managed to look so contrite that he had to remind himself she was an actress, the discovery he'd so painfully made.

"Sorry isn't enough, not for me, Jill, honey," he growled. He spun her around and with one quick motion tore open the buttons that ran down the back of the dress.

"What are you doing?" Jill cried out.

"Getting you ready to go on," Fargo said, and yanked the dress down, pulled it from her, and ignored her efforts to rake his face with her nails. He yanked her bloomers off while he held her struggling form with one hand and pushed her naked to the floor. He pulled the belt from a nearby bathrobe and tied her wrists with it.

"Stop it, damn you," Jill protested as she tried to struggle free, but he pushed her down again, one hand on her round rear. "The curtain's going up in a minute. I have to go on," she said.

"Oh, you're going on, all right, Jill, honey," he said. He glanced about and saw a silk kerchief on the makeup table. He reached over, pulled it down, and tied it around her mouth. Her protests were suddenly muffled screams as he lifted her up, tossed her over his shoulder, and strode from the dressing room with her. He went down the narrow corridor, and a silver-haired man in a frock coat appeared in the passage.

"What are you doing back here? Put that girl down at once," the man said.

Fargo brought one hand up, put it into the man's face, and pushed. The man disappeared in a crash of boxes and barrels. The Trailsman strode forward with Jill Foster, stepped onto the stage, and deposited her on the sofa. While she pushed herself into a sitting position, he peered through the break in the curtain. The audience was in place, the theater full, and he turned back to see Jill trying to rise and run. He caught her and flung her back onto the sofa. He tore the kerchief from her mouth and saw the horrified protest in her eyes as he yanked at the rope and brought the curtain up.

"Oh, God," Jill gasped as she looked out at the audience.

Fargo smiled, first at the shocked gasp that rose from the crowd as they stared at Jill's naked form and then at the utter horror on Jill's pretty face.

She tried to turn, bring her knees up in an attempt at salvaging some modesty, but he put one hand on her shoulder and yanked her back. "Ladies and gents, I give you Miss Jill Foster, that great actress," he announced to the shocked audience. "I bring her to you in the costume in which she does her very best acting." He bowed to the audience with a last flourish of his hand to Jill and strode from the stage with the rising murmur of the audience following him.

"No! Drop the curtain," Jill screamed after him, but he kept walking, strode out of the side door of the theater.

He returned to the Ovaro and rode from town, the anger still churning inside him. He finally slowed down and let the calm of the night work its effects. When he turned the pinto back toward Wellsville; he felt only the residue of his anger, but he took an unabashed satisfaction in what he'd done. She deserved every bit of it, he grunted even as he realized he'd changed nothing. She had plunged him into the middle of something he knew little about, and he was still there. He grunted with an edge of bitterness, reached Wellsville, and stopped at the dance hall for a bourbon and then returned to the inn and the comfort of the room.

His discovery about Jill had left a sourness inside him, and he undressed, turned down the lamp, and waited for sleep to push away the world. But instead of sleep, he sat up as the door shook with the fierce pounding against it. He pulled on trousers, opened the door, and stepped back as Jill Foster stormed into the room.

She wore the same deep green dress as on the first

day he'd met her, and she looked just as lovely, he noted with anger. "Damn you, Fargo," she spit out.

"How'd you find me?" he asked.

"Same way I found you that first time, your Ovaro outside," she said.

"You give a good performance tonight?"

"I was fired, damn you," Jill Foster flung back. "That man you shoved in the face was the producer. He said that I wasn't any use to him after tonight and that he put on legitimate plays for proper audiences, not exhibitions of naked women."

"You'll find another producer," Fargo said.

"You ruined me with that company, maybe with every traveling theater company. News travels fast. You might have ruined my career," Jill accused.

"Go east. There are lots of theater companies back East," Fargo said.

"With what? I've no money and no job and no way to go back East," she said. "All thanks to you, Skye Fargo."

"You've a convenient memory, Jill, honey. You can blame yourself. You did the lying," he said. "And I'm not interested in any more so you can waltz your little ass out of here."

"Well, there is more. There were a couple of roughnecks in the back seats. We get them sometimes. They were waiting when I left. They said they were going to give me a real chance to act for them. I managed to run away from them, but they followed me here," she said. Fargo's smile was patient skepticism. "Look out the window, damn you," Jill shouted.

He went to the window, parted the edge of the curtain, and his lips pursed. Two men were lounging across from the entrance, plainly waiting. "They're your problem, honey," he said coldly. "You sweet-talked me into doing what you wanted. Do the same with them." He moved past her and sat down on the bed.

"You're really being a bastard," she said.

"That always happens when I've been tricked into putting my neck in a noose by sweet-talking lies."

She whirled and went to the door, stopped there to look back at him. "You were wrong about one thing, you know," she said with an injured air.

"What's that?"

"What you said about doing my best acting when I'm naked," she answered. "I wasn't acting then."

"If you say so." He shrugged, unwilling to tell her he believed that much. She frowned back, yanked the door open, and strode out of the room.

Fargo waited, let her have a half-minute, and then rose and stepped to the window. He peered down to the street as she emerged from the inn, and he saw the two men immediately cross over to intercept her. He watched her halt, talk to the two men, and suddenly try to run. One seized her, clapped a hand over her mouth, and both began to drag her in between two buildings.

"Shit," Fargo bit out as he whirled, crossed the room in two long strides, and bolted down the hallway and out into the street. The town was still, streets deserted, as he ran down the space between the buildings. He didn't want a shoot-out if it could be avoided. Wellsville undoubtedly had a sheriff who might be stiff-backed.

He heard Jill's struggles and angry oaths before he reached the end of the passage, slowing to a halt to see the two men had tossed her into a half-empty hay wagon parked without its team. Both men were in the wagon, trying to pin Jill down as she struggled, both completely concentrated on their efforts.

Fargo swung up into the wagon over the closed tailgate, curled his hand around the shoulder of the nearest man, pulled him back, and half-lifted him up before smashing a roundhouse right to his jaw. The man arched backward, hit the side of the wagon, and flipped over and out.

Fargo turned to see surprise on the second man's beefy face turn to fury as the rapist stepped over Jill, seemed to start to throw a left. The Trailsman raised one arm to deflect the blow when the man suddenly dived low. Taken by surprise, Fargo tried to twist away, slipped on the hay, and the man crashed into him at the knees. Fargo felt himself go down and backward to smash against the tailgate with his shoulders. He swore as the gate flew open and he felt himself go out of the wagon, the man still wrapped around his legs.

He hit the ground on his back and the pain shot through him, but he felt the man's grip loosen around his knees. He pulled his legs up, kicked out, and the man rolled away to avoid a smashed face. Shoulders still aching, Fargo pushed to his feet in time to see the man charging again in another low dive. This time the Trailsman managed to twist away and brought a chopping blow down along the man's head as he flew past. He saw the man half-stumble, almost fall, catch himself, and whirl around with a line of red along the side of his face. The man charged again, abruptly halted, and shot out a looping right and a left that Fargo barely managed to pull away from in time. The man's beefy face a grimace, he started two more blows and once again switched to a low dive. The moves were his way of catching his opponents by surprise, Fargo realized, but he was ready this time. He stayed in place and brought a short, hard left hook up; it caught the diving figure flush on the jaw.

The man fell forward, arms half around Fargo's legs, but there was no strength in them now. He slid to his knees, shook his head, and started to get up before Fargo's blow drove downward against his cheekbones. The man toppled forward onto his face and lay still, his cheekbone a torn gash in the dirt.

Fargo spun as he heard the footsteps charging at him: the first man had recovered enough to return to the fight. He shot out a left that caught the man over the eye and sent an immediate spurt of red flowing downward. The man slowed, pawed at his eye, and Fargo's right hook caught him full on the jaw. He flew backward, smashed into the side of the hay wagon, and slowly slid to the ground.

Fargo looked up to see Jill still inside the wagon and waited as she jumped down from the opened tailgate. he turned and started to walk away.

"Wait," she called, and ran up to him. "You came after me," she said, eyes searching his face.

"Forget it," he said gruffly.

"Why? Guilty conscience?"

"Hell, no."

"What, then?" she persisted.

"I knew a mare once, sneaky and mean. You couldn't trust her a damn bit. She'd bite or kick whenever she felt like it. I still didn't want to see her become cougar meat," he said.

"You certainly know how to make something nice sound awful." She whirled and strode up the darkened street.

"Special talent," he called after her. "Like acting."

She refused to look back.

He chuckled as he returned to his room, stretched out, and embraced sleep.

5

He slept late, finally rose, and enjoyed the luxury of a hot bath. When he dressed and went outside, he found the morning well past the midway mark. He went to the dance-hall saloon, where he breakfasted on buckwheat cakes and good strong coffee. Finished, he took the Ovaro to the town stable and had the horse bathed, groomed, and fed.

He returned to the dance hall later in the day and found a poker game he could join. It was a good game, an amiable set of players with no cardshark involved, and he enjoyed himself and managed to lose only a few dollars. When he cashed in his chips, the night had grown late. None of the saloon girls was more than mildly tempting, and he realized he welcomed the quiet and relaxation more than he'd expected. All the long trail days were catching up at once, he recognized as he returned to the hotel room, undressed, and quickly slept.

When morning came, he decided he'd had enough of relaxation. Besides, it was time to start back to Standish. He breakfasted, went to the stable, and collected the Ovaro. The sun was in the midday sky when he rode from Wellsville. He had just left the town when he heard the hoofbeats behind him. He turned in the saddle, reined to a stop, and frowned at the rider who came alongside him.

"Finally leaving town?" Jill Foster remarked.

"What do you want?" Fargo growled, and took in her white blouse, scoop-necked, with breasts rising up over the neckline, her tan jodhpurs and matching boots. "Except for the saddle you could be in some girl's riding school back East" he commented.

"I spent the last of my money for this horse and saddle," Jill said. "Then I stood back watching you enjoy yourself all day yesterday."

"Why?" he asked.

"I was waiting for you to leave. I'm going with you."

"Hell you are."

"Hell I'm not," she snapped back. "I can't ride this country alone, not with all the Apache around. You get me to a town where I can find some work to earn enough to buy me a stage ticket east."

"You can do that in Wellsville," Fargo said.

"No, I can't. It's still small town. Everybody's heard what happened the other night. Either they don't want any part of me, or they want too much of me," Jill said, and a flash of frustration and helplessness touched her face. "That's all your doing, dammit," she added, almost in a pout, and he shrugged but silently admitted she was right. "I won't be a bother. I'll just tag along," she said. "I might even be good company."

"I'm not riding out. I'm going back to Herb Standish," he told her, and saw surprise and dismay cross her face. "He won't pay me the balance till I take him to Uvalde Flats."

"The balance was due on delivering the girl," she said.

"He claims you misunderstood him. I don't like turning away from what's due me over a few days more trailbreaking."

Jill frowned in thought for a moment. "Guess I ride along with you till you're finished." She shrugged.

"I don't think Standish is going to like me showing up with you," Fargo said.

72

"Then I'll just follow. It's a free country."

"Standish won't stand for that, either. And I don't like being followed." Fargo let himself reflect for a moment more. She'd brought it on herself, yet part of her predicament was his doing, he admitted. Maybe it wouldn't be all bad, he murmured to himself, and the memory of his first meeting with her kept intruding. "Let's ride," he said. "You get out of line and I'll leave you hanging on a saguaro."

He ignored her quick smile and put the pinto into a slow trot. He set an unhurried pace and was glad Jill knew the value of silence.

The day was beginning to near an end when he came into sight of Jonah. He rode through the town slowly yet consumed only three minutes, and it was he who finally broke the silence as he climbed the rock-strewn hill toward Standish's place. "What do you know about Standish?" he asked.

"Nothing. He saw me in the play and came to me afterward," she said.

"The girl's not his daughter," Fargo said, and drew a glance of surprise from her. "Stepdaughter. I'm wondering what he wants with her. Did he say anything to you?"

"No, and I didn't ask. I thought it best that way."

"She's going along with him, but not because she's happy about it," Fargo said. "I don't like the way the whole thing smells."

"You think she's in danger?"

"Not exactly, yet I wouldn't put bets on anything."

"She's just a kid, isn't she?" Jill inquired, and Fargo made no reply as the oversized cabin came into sight.

"This is it," he muttered, and she peered forward as he led the way into the clearing.

Jill had barely dismounted when Standish burst from the house. "What are you doing here?" he barked at her.

"She's with me," Fargo answered. "She'll ride along till I get her to a town where she can find a job."

"You won't be going through any towns," the man snapped curtly.

"I'll wait till he does," Jill cut in, and Fargo saw Clare step from the house, glance at him and then at Jill.

"I told you to get out of this part of the country," Standish barked at Jill.

"We finished our business. I don't have to take any more orders from you," Jill said.

"She rides along," Fargo said quietly, but Standish quickly caught the steel in his voice.

"You want to ride along you'll take orders," the man snapped at Jill. "Can you cook?"

"Yes," Jill said.

"Good, you'll do all the cooking. You can stay in the extra room tonight," Standish said, and he brought his eyes to Fargo. "The general sent the proper agreement. We'll be leaving tomorrow," he said, turned, and stalked into the house.

Clare stayed a moment, disapproval in the glance she threw at Fargo, and then returned into the house.

"Who's she?" Jill asked.

"The stepdaughter I took from the train," Fargo said, and saw Jill's jaw drop open.

"I thought she was just a kid," she murmured.

"So did I. We were both wrong."

She gave him a slanting glance. "Now I see why you're so concerned over her."

"Don't get smart," Fargo growled. "You heard the man's terms. It's his show. You want to stay?"

"There's not much I can do about it, is there?"

"Look at it as an experience. You might have to play a cook sometime," he said.

"Very funny," she threw back, and proceeded to take her things into the house.

Fargo saw Lew Baskins pass and exchanged nods with the man. He began to unsaddle the Ovaro.

Clare came outside again, the tightness still in her face. "I didn't expect you'd come back with your own private playmate."

"I'm doing her a favor, a good deed," he said.

"I'm sure you are," Clare said tartly.

He studied her face, the pale-lemon hair and eyebrows to match, the soft pink glow of her skin, and he wondered how all the pastel delicacy of her could suddenly look so cool. "You're sounding jealous, Clare, honey," he said.

"Nonsense," she snapped. "I just don't think you can pay proper attention to what you're here to do with your mind on your girlfriend."

"She's not my girlfriend and I can do more than one thing at a time," he said. "Besides, since when are you so concerned about what I do?"

"I thought I might help you help me," she said.

"That's talking in circles."

"I'll be more direct when the time comes," she said. "I'd just like to count on all your talents, not just a part of them."

"I'll tell you that after you start talking," he said.

She nodded, kept her face set tightly, and walked back to the house.

Fargo unsaddled the Ovaro, had supper with Lew Baskins and the other men in the bunkhouse, and when they turned in for the night, he carried his bedroll outside the perimeter of the clearing.

The big cabin grew dark and stillness cloaked the night. He saw the figure step from the cabin and come toward him on tentative steps. He rose and waved. Jill saw him and came toward him; she sank onto his bedroll with tiredness in her movements.

"This being a cook is for the birds, especially when I have to do all the cleaning up, too," she muttered.

"You come all the way out here to complain?"

"That and something else," Jill said. "I've been watching the girl."

"She has a name. Clare. You must know that by now," Fargo cut in.

Jill shrugged and went on quickly. "Well, delicate little Clare knows what Standish is up to. I think she's part of it."

"Could be because she's got no choice," Fargo said.

"Could be because she wants to be part of it," Jill said. "And she wants to make you a part of it. I saw the way she watched you from the window."

"That's not for you to bother about, honey," he said.

"I don't want to see you get into something more than you can handle."

"I'll remember that."

Jill rose and paused before him. "I'll see that you do," she snapped firmly, and strode back to the cabin.

He stretched out on his bedroll and wondered if there was ever a way to predict the behavior of a woman. He slept quickly, still wondering.

Morning came and he rose, went to the bunkhouse, and used the water barrel to wash. He dressed quickly and had the Ovaro saddled when Standish left the cabin, Clare beside him.

Lew Baskins brought their horses forward and Fargo saw Jill ride from behind the bunkhouse leading a pack mule loaded with supplies and cooking utensils.

"Your show now, Fargo," Standish said, and Fargo glanced at Clare. Her return glance was polite and contained.

The Trailsman sent the Ovaro into a canter and left the others to follow him west across a rocky hillside. He rode on, scouted the terrain, and found it filled with passages and trails among rock formations and black oak stands. He headed directly west, halted often enough for the others to glimpse him and follow.

The day passed easily and they made good time. He noted a half-dozen trails of Apache ponies but none less than a few days old. When night came, he found a place to camp among a rock clearing. He ate with the others as Jill dished out hot beans and buffalo strips. He finished last and bestowed a wide smile on her as she collected his plate. "Mighty wonderful, honey," he said. "This might be a new career for you."

"Eat your words," she muttered, and strode away.

When the others bedded down, Fargo took his bedroll up to a high ledge that let him look down on the campsite and out across the distant terrain. He undressed to his underdrawers, stretched out on one elbow, and let his eyes scan the moonlit distances. He was listening to the howl of a red wolf somewhere in the terraced hills and valleys when he caught the flicker of movement in the camp below.

A figure moved around the edge of the rocks and hurried toward the narrow path that led to the ledge where he waited. The figure climbed, came closer, became a blue robe and soft dark brown hair.

"You saw me come up here," Fargo said.

"Yes, I was awake and watching," Jill said.

"Why?" he asked.

"I told you I'd keep you out of trouble," she said, sinking down on the bedroll.

"How do you figure to do that up here?"

"This way," she said, and pulled the robe open to reveal that she wore absolutely nothing beneath. With a shake of her shoulders, the rest of the robe dropped away, and his eyes took in the beautifully curved breasts, memory instantly returning as he gazed at the lean rib cage, smooth abdomen, and narrow hips that were without an extra ounce of flesh.

Jill leaned forward, arms circling his neck, and he felt himself responding instantly as her nipples rubbed against his chest, tiny pressure points of firm softness that sent a shiver through him.

"I can't forget that one time, Fargo," she breathed. "It's stayed with me ever since."

Her legs came forward, parted, and she sank atop him, twisting her pelvis to find his upright waiting. He felt the warm moistness of her as she brought herself down over him, sank to the very end of her liquescent tunnel, the soft wall touching against him.

"Aaaaah, aaaaah," Jill breathed, pressing harder. She drew back and pressed down again, sweet softness enveloping him, her lean thighs clasped hard against his hips. She slid up and down, slow pumping that began to grow faster. "Ah, Jesus, ah, ah, aaaaah," Jill gasped. She brought her swaying breasts down to his face, found his open lips, pressed deep into his mouth. She moaned as her hips bounced up and down on him, faster and faster, and he felt her nipples push hard against his tongue. He saw her lift her head, her neck stretched upward, her own mouth open in gasping moans as she pumped furiously, slowed, increased speed again, and then slowed. He felt the pumping contractions of his own organ keep pace with her and then begin to spiral beyond his control.

Pleasure refused denial, ecstasy refused to stay its explosion, and then he saw Jill's head raise skyward, her neck stretch upward, and she screamed into the night as her buttocks and pubic mound quivered atop him. She pressed hard, held for that instant of eternity, and then her scream died away, became a series of broken gasps until she collapsed over him and lay still, her skin bonded to his, breasts pressed over his face. Finally, with a last quivering sigh, she fell away from him to lay alongside him, one lean thigh still draped across his belly.

He let his gaze rove across her spent beauty, the full-cupped breasts rising and falling with each deep breath she drew, her lean body a limp wire drained of its electric current. She turned, curled against him, and he let her half-nap, satisfied and emptied.

But finally she rose onto one elbow, gray eyes open wide, a faint smile toying with her lips. "How does this keep me out of trouble?" he asked. "Seems the other way around."

"It'll keep you satisfied. You won't be so easy a mark for little Clare," Jill said.

"Maybe," he said, and studied her face. "And maybe it's really something else."

"Such as?"

"Making sure I keep you along."

She sat up and pulled the robe on indignantly. "That's a rotten thing to say."

"Lots of rotten things are true."

"Well, not that one. I'm thinking of your good," she said, pushed to her feet, and stood over him. "You'll see." She turned and hurried down the path back to the camp.

He watched from the ledge, saw her lie down on her blanket, and sat back and stretched out on his own bedroll. Whatever her motives, selfish or unselfish or just plain female jealousy, she might make an arduous trip less so, he decided as he closed his eyes in sleep.

When morning came, he rose, readied himself, and returned to the campsite below. He took a cup of coffee from Jill, sipped it slowly while the others prepared to ride.

Clare spoke to everyone but him, passed by twice without a glance, and he felt curiosity more than anything else. But he also knew he'd not give her the satisfaction of responding.

Fargo saddled the Ovaro and led the way west, riding on ahead of the others. He found a long, downward lay in the land, rock and thick brush along the sides, and enough Indian pony prints to make him cautious. He kept a steady pace till past noon when he reached a stream at the end of the long lay of land. There he halted and let the Ovaro drink as the others finally caught up.

He had scouted the land ahead and found a trail that ran level on land that sloped up on both sides, and when the others had rested enough, he spoke to Standish.

"Move on along the trail. I'll be riding the high land and meet up with you later," he said, and sent the pinto into a trot that took him across the nearest slope. He didn't hurry, and even slowed when he reached the higher land. He scanned the distant terrain and saw nothing to cause alarm. He walked on over the ridged land when he heard the sound of hoofbeats coming up behind him, a single horse, and he turned and caught the flash of lemon-blond hair in the afternoon sun. She rode up to him, gray eyes still cool, her lips tight.

"Standish know you're up here?" Fargo asked.

"No. I told him I just wanted to ride alone some. I didn't give him chance to argue about it," she said.

"This isn't riding alone," he commented.

"You said she wasn't your private playmate," Clare tossed at him. "I happened to wake just as she came back to her blanket last night."

"You're sounding jealous again, Clare, honey," he said evenly.

"I told you that's nonsense," she snapped, and glared at his smile. "I just have to know something."

"I don't think that's any of your business," he said.

"Not that." She frowned angrily. "I have to know if I can count on you or if you're more interested in taking off with your playmate as soon as we get to the Uvalde Flats."

"You're still sounding jealous."

A faint flush touched her pastel coloring. "Forget how I sound and answer me."

"Start leveling with me and I'll answer you. What's this all about? What's this pact between Standish and the general? Where do the Mexicans fit in? Where do you fit in? Talk if you want answers from me," he said harshly.

"I don't know where to start," she said.

"Try Standish and a hundred Mexican soldiers and the general," Fargo said.

"Some years ago, Standish and General de los Santos made plans to take Texas back, to make it into a separate republic again," Clare said, and Fargo felt the furrow slide across his brow. "They have all the details worked out. Standish will be president, but the real power will lay in Mexico with de los Santos."

"That's ridiculous," Fargo said.

"Not any longer," Clare said. "They're going to take advantage of the fact that the Union armies and the southern forces are preparing for possible war. Federal troops have been pulled back to the Mason-Dixon Line except for a few contingents left. Confederate leaders in Texas are sending their troops north out of the state and up to Virginia. Standish and General de los Santos have recognized that there's a military vacuum in Texas, and they're going to take advantage of it. Once they establish a new republic Standish can ask for Mexican aid."

The furrow on Fargo's brow had become a deep trench as he realized the very real truth in what Clare had said. It seemed impossible, ridiculous, yet suddenly it was anything but a wild idea. "Big talk and big plans are one thing. Putting them into effect is another," he said. "That takes men, action, materials."

"They're ready with those things. Standish and the general are crazy men, but they're also very determined and very practical. They wouldn't be the first crazy men to succeed at things others laughed at," she said.

He grimaced and again knew the chilling truth in her words.

"Standish has three hundred American mercenaries

gathering at the Uvalde Flats. The general is supplying a thousand Mexican soldiers."

"Jesus," Fargo murmured, and let a low whistle pass his lips. "You're sure about all this?"

"Very sure. That's where I come in. Standish has to supply his mercenaries with arms, ammunition, and good horses. My grandfather left me a great deal of money I can draw on, but only through American banks. I can't draw on it from Mexico."

"So he has to have you here in the States, where he can use you and control you," Fargo said, and she nodded.

"He has the checks and vouchers for me to sign to pay for all the things he needs," she said.

"And if you don't go along with it?"

"It will be bad for my mother," Clare said. "The general told me that, and Standish too. I have to go along."

Fargo halted and swung to the ground, his brow deep with furrows as he stared out across the distant terrain. He went over everything Clare had told him, all the wild and unbelievable craziness of it, and again it came down to one frightening truth: it was possible. Standish and the Mexican general had hold of enough factors to make it work. Once they established their new republic, the Mexicans, under de los Santos, could rush in to solidify the new regime and do it legally. They'd simply be going to the aid of a new independent country that had asked for their help. Ordinarily, in normal times, it wouldn't stand a chance of working. But these were not normal times. The dark clouds of possible war occupied the resources and attentions of the established forces of the North and the gathering forces of the South. They were very right. There was a military vacuum, and they'd take advantage of it.

"Where and when is all this supposed to happen?" Fargo asked, turning back to Clare.

"When the mercenaries are fully equipped and all the supplies are in hand, Standish will march south to a spot just below Eagle Pass. De los Santos will cross the border there and hook them up with his main force. He'll have smaller forces taking over a dozen border towns," Clare said. "But the main meeting will be between de los Santos and Standish below Eagle Pass. That's where Standish will announce the new Republic of Texas."

"Just what do you expect I can do, Clare?" Fargo frowned. "You talk about helping you. How?"

"I don't know how exactly, but I want to stop them. I thought if we worked together we might find a way. I'll know what supplies are coming and when. I'll have to sign the vouchers for them. I can tell you," she said.

"And what am I supposed to do, then? Dig a hole for them to fall into?"

"Don't you want to stop this?" Clare asked accusingly.

" 'Want' isn't the word. Try how," he flung back.

"Maybe you'll find a way. That's what I'm hoping," she said. "I want to stop Standish and de los Santos. They both grow on the same rotten vine."

He reached out, took her by the shoulders, and suddenly she was against him, lemon hair brushing his face, a tiny tremor going through her body. "I'd like to blow this apart," he told her. "I'd like to find a way. I'm just not sure it's possible. But with your help, maybe I can find a way. I'll sure try."

"If I help you find a way, will you do something for me?" she asked, lifting her face to him.

"What?"

"I'll tell you when the time comes."

"Why not?" he said.

She lifted her hands, put them against his cheeks, and held his face for a long moment, then stepped back. "Good," she said. "Now you see why I had to

83

know if you were just waiting to run off with Jill Foster."

"I might've been. This puts a different face on everything," he said.

"I'd best get back to Standish now," she said, lifted her face to the sun for a moment, and let a deep sigh lift her breasts to press into her blouse. She turned and climbed onto the horse with a graceful motion.

"You going to tell Standish that you told me about his plans?"

"Not now. Maybe when we reach Uvalde Flats. Or maybe he'll tell you himself, then," she said.

He nodded agreement and watched her ride back the way she had come. He swung onto the pinto and stayed on the high land until dusk began to slide along the tall rocks. He rode down, then, met the others where the trail split in two directions. He chose the one that curved west, and found a spot to camp before darkness descended.

The supper meal was the same as the night before, and everyone ate quickly. When Fargo started to take his bedroll into a stand of black oak a dozen yards away, Herb Standish called to him.

"Why do you always go off by yourself, Fargo?" the man asked.

"I've always done it. Anything unexpected happens, I'm in a better spot to react," Fargo answered.

Standish gave him an appraising stare. "I could use a man like you, Fargo," he said. "Would you think of staying on after we reach Uvalde Flats?"

"Depends what for," Fargo said.

"Of course. I'll give you more details when the time comes," Standish said, and Fargo nodded politely, letting his eyes pass across Clare as she sat nearby. She smiled with cool formality, but he caught the moment that flashed in her eyes.

He went on into the trees and set down his things.

He couldn't begin to make plans until he reached the Uvalde, he knew, but the first move had been made. He'd have to stay on to find a time and a place, if anything became possible at all. It was a beginning, but one that might never grow to be anything more, he realized darkly. He lay on his bedroll and his thoughts raced as the night deepened. He heard the soft footsteps moving through the trees and sat up. "Over here," he called, and Jill appeared in a moment, the robe wrapped around herself.

"I had to wait for everyone to get to sleep," she said.

"Doesn't make much difference. Clare saw you go back to your blanket last night," he said.

"Did she, now?" Jill smiled and sat down beside him. "What else did she have to say to you this afternoon?"

"How do you know she was with me?" Fargo asked in surprise, and Jill tossed him a chiding half-smile.

"I didn't believe that wanting-to-ride-alone story for a damn second. Neither did Standish," she said.

"What makes you think that?" Fargo frowned.

"It was in his eyes as he watched her go. Besides, if he thought she was really going to roam around alone, he'd never have let her go. He's no fool, and she underestimates him," Jill said.

"I doubt that. And maybe he's no fool, but he's a madman," Fargo said. "But I have to wonder if he expected she'd tell me the things she did, now, especially after the question he tossed at me when I left camp."

"What things?" Jill asked, and Fargo leaned back on one elbow and quickly recounted everything Clare had told him.

Jill Foster's eyes were wide when he finished and she let out a deep breath. "Jesus," she murmured.

"Exactly," Fargo grunted.

"You're not going to go along with her, are you?"

"Seems like the right thing to do," he muttered.

"Seems like shit to me," Jill snapped. "You can't do anything about this. You'll just get yourself killed."

"This isn't something a man can turn away from," Fargo said. "Not if he cares about his country."

"Standish isn't the madman. You are," Jill said angrily. "Besides, she's only using you because she wants to wreck the whole scheme. She wants to get back at Standish and the general, and she can't do it alone."

He turned the words in his mind. "Maybe that's part of it. Maybe those are her real reasons. But that doesn't change things any," he said.

"Why not?"

"If a house is on fire, people can have their own reasons for trying to put out the fire. The important thing is that the fire is put out."

"Not by killing yourself trying," she snapped. "Dammit, Fargo, I don't want to be stranded alone while you get yourself killed doing something you can't do."

"Seems to me your reasons are just as selfish as you say hers are."

"Not the same way, dammit. I want you alive. I want you to be able to make love to me."

"You didn't feel this way when you sent me out to take her from a hundred Mexican soldiers and made up that sob story to get me to do it," he reminded her, and her lips tightened for an instant.

"That was then. This is now," she said. "I want you, the man, alive and with me. She wants you the hero, alive or dead."

"I'll think some more on it," he told her when she tore the robe open, brought her nakedness against him with a kind of savagery, her hands seeking, finding his instant response.

"This'll help your thinking," she murmured, and let

passion and flesh consume the night until she finally lay beside him, her breasts heaving with deep, satisfied gasps.

He held her, caressed her into rest, and when she finally returned to the camp, he lay awake and wondered about the differences in selfishness. Jill's was all personal fire, all from deep inside and wrapped in a kind of caring she believed changed everything about it. Clare's was wrapped in a less personal cloth, revenge clothed with a cloak of idealism. Did the wrapping make the difference? Or was it just two sides of the same coin?

He turned onto his side and embraced sleep, aware that the question was one wise men could ponder over the ages. He had more practical things to face, such as the odds of success and the price of failure. Fine words for life or death.

6

Jill served morning coffee with a mixture of apprehension and smugness in her face, Fargo noted. Clare wore only cool determination in her gray eyes as her pastel coloring shimmered in the early sun. His night thoughts returned. Differences, he grunted inwardly, and he had no doubt he'd find out how much they meant. Or how little, he added.

When they were ready to ride, he motioned them forward along the pathway and found Clare hurrying after him as he turned up to higher ground.

"I'll ride along some with you," she said.

"No excuses to Standish this morning?" Fargo asked.

"No," she said.

"Just as well. Jill's sure he figured you went up to see me yesterday. She thinks you underestimate him."

"I knew he'd think that. It's exactly what I wanted him to think. He's certain I like you and want you to like me, and he's already making use of that. He sent me to talk to you this morning," Clare said. "He wants me to get you to stay on. He needs men such as you."

Fargo's smile held wry admiration. Standish thought he was using her when it was really the other way around. He knew who was guilty of underestimating, and her name was Jill. "How much are you supposed to tell me?" he asked.

"Nothing. Just soften you up so's you'll want to stay," she said.

He rode to a small ledge that projected over the terrain below and swung to the ground. Clare dismounted and came to stand alongside him as he scanned the land in the distance. He turned to her, lifted one hand to cup her chin.

"Don't you want to work harder at your job?" he asked, and pressed his mouth on hers. His left hand went around her back and drew her to him as he continued to kiss her. She kept her lips firm, almost closed, but he pressed harder and suddenly her mouth half-opened, grew soft, and she returned his kiss. He pulled her tighter, felt the soft warm curve of her breasts against his chest, and then her hands were pushing against him and she tore away.

"No," she half-gasped, stared up at him with her gray eyes touched by panic. "That'll only complicate things," she said. "This is going to be difficult enough. I don't want to add more problems."

"That's a different kind of excuse." Fargo smiled and she stepped back, the faint flush coloring her face again.

"Different or not, it'll have to do," she said with too much quick anger. She turned and climbed onto her horse. "I'd best get back. No sense in overdoing it."

"No, we wouldn't want that." Fargo watched her ride off and move downhill until she disappeared from sight. He returned to the saddle and rode on.

The land grew flatter, the valleys wider, sandstone buttresses replaced by long, sloping hills and road-cut erosions. He watched a distant spiral of dust, turned away from it, and hurried down to meet the others to send them in a circular path south until it was safe to return west. As the day wore to a close, he guided the small band into a draw he had spotted from his scouting, one side a sandy-soiled slope, the other well-covered by laurel oak.

Night descended and supper was taken beside a small fire, Jill serving with unsmiling efficiency.

"We'll make the flats, come morning," Fargo told Standish, and saw the man beam in pleasure.

"You've done well, Fargo. Good riding, no problems, and we've made good time. But then you're the best," Standish said.

"Clare tells me you've big plans," Fargo said carefully. "I'll admit I'm curious."

"Good. We'll talk about them tomorrow," Standish said, and Fargo glimpsed Jill listening as she cleaned off the supper plates, her face set. Clare, her fine-featured face expressionless, rose to her feet, and Standish followed. "Time to get some sleep," the man said, and moved to the side of the draw.

Fargo took his bedroll from the Ovaro and started to walk toward the tree-covered slope when Jill whispered to him. "Where will you be?" she asked.

"In the laurel oak, by the tall tree that stands higher than the others," he said, and walked on.

The slope was a gentle climb, but the moonlight had to fight its way through the thickness of the foliage. He reached the tall oak, set his things down, and had just undressed to his trousers when he heard the figure hurrying up the slope. He was prepared for the anger in Jill's eyes when she reached him, the robe wrapped tightly around her.

"Dammit, Fargo, I couldn't believe my ears down there," she blurted out. "You're really going ahead with this, aren't you?"

"It's likely," he said, and she sank to her knees beside him.

"After all we talked about last night, and everything else?" she glowered.

"I'm afraid so, honey."

"Are you that taken with her?" Jill speared. "You want to get her in the sack that badly?"

"What's that got to do with it?"

"I can't think of any other reason that makes any sense," she snapped.

90

"Listen to me. Every once in a while a man's given the chance to think of something besides himself, to do something important. He turns his back and he has to live with that the rest of his life," he said. "This is one of those times."

She offered a disdainful glance. "How terribly lofty. I think you're doing it so Clare will be grateful enough to fall into bed with you," she said.

"God, you've a nasty little turn of mind, you know that?" Fargo said.

"I know men."

"Well, you're wrong this time around."

She fell silent, her lips tightened, and finally lifted her eyes to him. "You promise that's not it?"

"Promise," he said, and she half-rose, threw her arms around him.

"Dammit, Fargo, I'm scared, and you've become something special. I still say, Let's just leave, as fast as we can. Think about it again, please?" she implored.

"All right," he agreed, and the robe came open and she flung her warm nakedness against him.

"More convincing?"

"You object?" she returned as she rubbed her breasts against his chest.

"Hell, no!"

"Besides, there might not be a time or place after tomorrow," Jill said, and she proceeded to make the most of the opportunity, her wanting a driving, almost desperate desire.

The warm night became a place of exploding sensations, her cries muffled against his chest as he satisfied her every demand. Finally, her final ecstasy depleted, she lay in his arms. When she gathered herself to leave, the robe wrapped around her again, she clung to him a moment longer. "Be careful. Whatever you decide, be careful," she murmured.

"Count on it," he told her, and she pulled away and almost ran down the slope.

He slept quickly, rose early, and set a fast pace through the morning. It was just before noon when they reached the platelike flat lands set off in huge sections by borders of low rock forms. He saw the figures dotting the nearest stretch, close to a hundred at a quick count, he saw. Some had come in one-horse farm wagons, others in big, converted platform spring drays, but most by horse. Some had set up tarpaulin lean-to tents to get out from under the hot sun, but most lounged across the dry ground.

"The early ones. The others will be arriving within days," Standish said, his eyes shining with excitement.

Fargo stayed back as he rode out into the men who rose to gather around him. Clare stayed back also, as Jill followed Lew Barkins and the others into the camp area.

Fargo saw Clare's eyes sweep the men and her lips thin. "There'll be another two hundred. The more I think about it, the more impossible it seems," she said. "And the more I know I have to try to stop it. You still want to help?"

"Yes," Fargo said. "You've wondered if I've had second thoughts?"

"Yes. I expect Jill Foster has been begging you to forget everything and run off with her," Clare said.

"You guessing, or did she tell you as much?" Fargo asked.

"Neither. It's what I'd expect of her," Clare said. "Maybe even of myself, were I in her shoes."

"That's honest enough," Fargo said. "I'm going to get a spot for myself. When do we talk again?"

"Tomorrow. It'll be easier. Standish will be busy with the new men coming in," she said.

Fargo nodded and moved away from her; he staked out a spot and slid from the horse. By the afternoon's end at least fifty more men had arrived, straggling in in small groups, a few arriving by wagon. He strolled among those who had already arrived, exchanged nods, and finally returned to his spot. They were all one of a kind, he had noted, hard-eyed, thin-lipped men, some scragglier than others, but he saw no derelicts and no young hotbloods to cause trouble. Standish had obviously recruited carefully and offered good money.

The day wore to an end and a dozen campfires appeared across the flat land. Standish returned to the front edge of the area and settled down while Lew Barkins started a fire for Jill to prepare supper.

"I'm getting tired of this," she announced as she served the meal.

"You won't need to do it much longer, my dear," Standish said. "The time for great things is getting closer." His mood was plainly confident and expansive as he turned to Fargo. "How'd you like to be a part of history, Fargo? How'd you like a chance to make history?"

"Guess everyone would like that," Fargo said blandly.

"I'm offering you that chance," Standish said. "I'm offering you the chance to make Texas an independent nation again."

Fargo let his brows lift in surprise and leaned closer.

Standish went on to detail his grand scheme, repeating everything Clare had told him with the added emphasis of grand dreams.

Once again, as he listened, Fargo felt the chill inside him and realized how possible it was for the plan to succeed, wild and improbable as it seemed. But this was a world where wild and improbable things had succeeded before because they came into being at the exact right moment. A year, a month, sometimes just a week too late or too early made things fail. The exact right time, that was the key to it, and Standish could be holding that key this time.

When the man finished, Fargo allowed himself to appear both impressed and astounded.

"You want to become part of it, Fargo? You'll get top dollar and a chance to make history," Standish finished.

Fargo let his lips purse in thought. He couldn't agree too easily. Standish had the kind of crafty mind that could seize on little things. He'd have to play the little things, too, Fargo pondered, and he let his eyes go to Clare, study her, and he knew Standish watched him closely. "What happens to Clare when you win?" he asked.

"She can return to Mexico and her mother," Standish said. "Or she can do whatever she likes."

In his explanation of the scheme he had carefully omitted Clare's role in it, Fargo had noted, and he half-shrugged as he took his gaze from her. "I want the two thousand you still owe me first. I like things neat," he said.

Standish smiled. "I wouldn't expect less of you," he said, pulled a roll of bills from his pocket, and handed them over. "Now, will you be part of it?" he pressed.

"Why not?" Fargo said. "I always thought that Texas is too big to be just another state. It ought to be its own nation. Sam Houston had the right idea."

"Good." Standish beamed. "We'll need every good man we can get. We'll go over your assignment in the morning."

"Fair enough," Fargo said, and he rose to his feet. He took his bedroll and walked to the perimeter of the campsite, where he undressed and stretched out. He expected no visitors and received none and was glad for it. He lay awake for an hour after the campsite grew still; he let his mind turn over possibilities and options and finally went to sleep wondering if Jill were right about his being a fool.

He dressed with the morning sun and returned to where Standish waited and sipped a tin cup of coffee.

Jill handed him a cup, disdain in her glance.

"You'll start doing what you do best, Fargo," Standish said. "Scout the land in all directions. I don't want anyone coming near this area. I'm not worried about the Apache. I don't expect they'd attack a force this size."

"Don't be too sure," Fargo said, and Standish frowned.

"There are Apache main camps that can send out over three hundred warriors, maybe some close by," Fargo told him.

"All right, that's all the more reason for you to scout," Standish said. "The more likely thing is a cattle drive coming too close, or a wagon train. I want you to alert me if that happens, and we'll disperse until they go by. The important thing is I don't want anyone seeing this force while we're waiting for supplies. People carry stories. The wrong ears could hear them."

"That's right. It pays to be careful," Fargo agreed. "I'll start riding out now."

"I'll send Lew and Sam White out with you," Standish said.

"I scout alone," Fargo said.

"Just for a day or two, until you get into the routine." Standish smiled.

Fargo shrugged. "You're the boss," he said, and saw Standish look pleased. When the man walked away and went out to stroll through the campsite as still more arrivals appeared, Fargo found Clare beside him. "He doesn't trust me yet. That's why the nursemaids."

"He's not much for trusting," Clare said. Her hand came up to press against his arm. "I may have something for you to work on tomorrow."

He nodded and climbed onto the Ovaro, walked the horse past where Jill threw a narrow-eyed glance up at him.

"Principles, not pussy, remember," she muttered.

"That's what I said," he answered.

"That's what you promised," she corrected.

He nodded and moved on. Lew Barkins rode up to fall alongside him and the other man drew up a few paces behind. Fargo rode from the flat land, across the low rock forms that bordered the flats, and moved westward, his eyes narrowed as he scanned the dry terrain. A grim smile curled inside him. Standish was concerned over being seen by stray wagon trains and cattle drives, with some concern over the Apache. He was succumbing to overconfidence, Fargo noted inwardly. Perhaps there was more than he counted on. Of course, that lay in things beyond his control, Fargo realized, in the shadow of luck and the promise of hope. He'd ride holding both.

He set out over the flat land and quickly reached the rock formations of the little hills where black oak and cottonwoods mingled with sandstone buttresses. Lew Barkins and Sam White kept slightly behind as he rode and turned in a slow circle from west to south. When afternoon came, he moved east. They were as he'd said, merely watchdogs. They saw little and recognized less, unaware even of the unshod pony tracks that moved over the high ridge in sizable groups. Hunting parties, the Trailsman grunted, some dragging their catch behind them. But there were plenty of them, and they converged at an uneven ridge before moving down the other side. It was plain the Apache had a major camp beyond the ridge.

It was only when the afternoon had begun to wane that Barkins noted the column of dust that moved toward them and that Fargo had been watching for a half-hour.

"Over there, Apache," Barkins said, alarm in his voice.

"No," Fargo said.

"How the hell do you know that?" Barkins snapped.

"Too much dust. Horses wearing shoes. Dust column holding too steady," Fargo said. He kept his face impassive as the hope exploded inside him. He moved into a crevice of the rock, and Barkins and White followed as he kept his eyes on the column of dust. Suddenly it moved behind rocks, emerged on the other side as a double line of blue-uniformed horsemen in a neat column of twos. An officer headed the column, the platoon flag carried behind him.

"Shit. The cavalry," Barkins spit out. "They're heading right for the camp." He started to wheel his horse around. "We've got to get back and warn Standish."

"Why?" Fargo asked, pulling him back into the crevice.

"Why?" Barkins asked, incredulousness in the single word. "So he can get everybody the hell out of sight."

"That won't help much. This is a trained cavalry patrol. They'll pick up the marks, burned campfire logs, footprints, hoofprints, a lot of everything. They'll know something's going on," Fargo said.

"Then we get back and tell Standish so's he can wipe them out. I don't figure there's more than fifty of them," Barkins said.

Fargo shook his head again, his eyes on the patrol that drew closer. The squeeze was suddenly pressing at him. He had two stories to sell, both designed to buy him time. "No good," he said to Barkins. "A patrol reports in, maybe tomorrow, maybe the next day. When it doesn't you can be sure they'll come looking," he said.

"Christ, we have to do something. Let's get back and let Standish decide," Barkins said.

"No time for that now. You two just back me up," Fargo said, and sent the Ovaro racing from the crevice. He heard the two men follow as he rode forward to meet the blue-uniformed column.

The officer brought his troopers to a halt as he saw the three men racing toward him.

"God, are we glad to see you," Fargo said, skidding the Ovaro to a halt.

"Major Nelson, Fourth U.S. Cavalry," the officer said.

"Apaches, riding south hard, about thirty of them," Fargo said. "They just missed us. But we saw a wagon train moving south about an hour ago. I think they're after it."

"Probably," the major barked. He rose in his saddle and shouted orders to his troops. The column turned south as Major Nelson sent his horse into a gallop.

Fargo watched them go until they disappeared, only the column of dust left in the air. "They'll search until it gets dark," he said. "Come morning, they'll stay south looking for the Apache and the wagon train." He wheeled the Ovaro, and the others fell in behind as he headed back to the flats at a fast canter.

Dark had come when they reached the campsite, the cooking fires dotting the site. Fargo found that Standish had moved his own area against the low rocks. He let Lew Barkins hurry to talk to Standish while he led the Ovaro to the side and saw Jill serving beans and bacon while Clare sat by the fire. He dismounted and strolled to where Standish beamed at him.

"The boys told me how you handled that cavalry patrol. That was really outstanding thinking, Fargo," Standish said. "I see I was right in bringing you in."

"You can do something," Fargo said flatly. "I ride alone from now on. I don't like company when I scout. I told you that."

"Yes, so you did. Of course. Whatever you want, Fargo," Standish said, happy to be accommodating.

"Good," Fargo said. He sat down and took a plate from Jill. He had scored with Standish. That was important, but the night held still more important things. He ate with the others and forced himself not to hurry, not to seem impatient, and when the meal was over, he lounged beside Clare. He rose only when he saw Standish begin to prepare for bed and he strolled past Jill on his way to the rocks.

"Where are you going to be later?" she whispered.

"No place you'll be visiting," he said.

"Why not?" She frowned at once. "You expecting somebody else?"

"No, dammit, but I'm expecting you to listen to me," he hissed back, and hurried on. He took his bedroll from the Ovaro as he always did and clambered up the low rocks to where he could see the campsite stretched out below. He sat down, but this time he didn't set out the bedroll. Instead, he leaned back against a rock, his gaze on the site below, and he waited, grim-faced, while the camp settled down.

With maddening slowness, the figures that dotted the land grew still, the fires burned out, and the moon had risen high when he finally moved down from the rocks. He went to the Ovaro, closed his hand around the cheek strap, and carefully led the horse along the edge of the rocks, skirting the sleeping figures, until he found a space and vanished into the rocks again. He climbed onto the horse when he was far enough from the campsite, and put the horse into a slow trot. Only when he'd cleared the other side of the rocks did he go into a gallop. He turned south and raced through the night, certain the cavalry had given chase for at least an hour.

Finally the Trailsman slowed and sent the pinto up atop a low hill that nonetheless let him peer forward through the moonlit terrain. Rock forms rose to his right, more to the left, and he concentrated his gaze on the long plateau in between. Suddenly he made out the low, dark shapes in the distance, and he sent the

Ovaro onto the plateau, raced on until the dark shapes took on form, became a line of horses tethered at one side and the prone shapes of sleeping figures with a field tent at one end.

He slowed as he neared the bivouac and saw that Major Nelson had put out sentries.

The two troopers faced him with carbines raised. "Come forward with your hands up," one called, and Fargo obeyed, halted at the edge of the camp. "Dismount," the sentry ordered, and again he obeyed.

"I want to see Major Nelson," Fargo said. The sentries exchanged glances and he saw some of the nearest figures sit up. "It's very important," the Trailsman pressed.

"Watch him," one sentry said, and hurried to the small field tent. He returned in a few moments with the major, who was still buttoning his uniform jacket.

Nelson halted and frowned at the visitor. "You're the one who told us about the Apache," the major said. "We didn't find them."

"That was a lie," Fargo said, and saw the man's eyes widen in astonishment.

"What's this mean, mister?" Major Nelson growled.

"Can we talk in your tent?" Fargo asked.

The major frowned in thought for a moment. "You two men come along," he ordered two of the troopers, and led the way back to the field tent. Inside, he lighted a hurricane lamp and waited, his jaw grim. "Start with your name," he snapped.

"Fargo, Skye Fargo."

"The Trailsman?" Major Nelson asked.

"They call me that," Fargo said. "I've worked with General Mitchell."

"Yes, it was the general who told me about you," the major said. "Quite a few stories, in fact. You say you lied about the Apache? I don't understand."

"Maybe you'd best sit down on your cot, Major,"

Fargo said. "I'm about to tell you the goddamnedest story you'll ever hear. You'll think I've had a cask of bourbon or that I'm plumb loco, but every word of it is true."

"Go on, Fargo," the officer said, and lowered himself to the edge of the cot.

Fargo began to recount everything Clare and Standish had told him of the scheme. He paced back and forth as he spoke and realized the telling of it didn't make it sound any less ridiculous. But he supplied details, times, places, and his own sense of desperate awe, and when he finished, he slumped down on the cot.

"Crazy, isn't it?" he muttered. "But every word of it's true." He held his gaze on the major's drawn face, saw the man's eyes stare hard at him.

"I wouldn't believe one damn word of this except for what General Mitchell's told me about you, Fargo," Major Nelson said. "But I've got to believe it. There's another reason. I don't think you could concoct a story like that one."

"You're right, I couldn't," Fargo said. "Worst of all, it can work. It will work unless you get to the general and move on this right away. If Standish and de los Santos get a real military foothold, they'll go from there."

"There may not be a damn thing we can do to stop it," the major said, and Fargo frowned back. "First, it'll take me days to reach General Mitchell. Second, he may not have enough men to do anything. Most of his command has been sent north. If he can scrape enough men together, it'll still take days for us to get back here. They could be established then and impossible to oust." His face drawn, the major rose and pulled a map out of a leather pouch beside the cot. He spread it open by the lamp and traced his finger along one section.

"Right there, just below Eagle Pass," Fargo said. "That's where de los Santos will cross the river with his main force and meet Standish."

"It's a wide valley with high land on both sides. It's the best place for the Mexican to bring his troops across the river that we call the Rio Grande and they call the Rio Bravo del Norte. If General Mitchell can get enough of a force together, we'll have to attack there," Major Nelson said, and folded the map closed. "You'll have to buy us time, Fargo, find a way to delay things as long as you can."

"I'll do my best," Fargo said grimly.

"I'd guess the Mexican won't cross into Texas until Standish arrives with his force," the major said. "If he did, it could be seen as a direct invasion and nothing more. But with Standish on the scene and establishing his new Republic of Texas, it'll technically be responding to a call for assistance. All legalities to have in place for any future challenge, but it means one important thing to us now: the Mexicans will wait until the American force reaches the meeting place before crossing over. That's why delaying Standish is vital."

"God knows how I can do it, but I'll sure try," Fargo said, and the major turned to the two troopers.

"Get the men up. We ride now," he said, and the soldiers hurried outside as he turned back to Fargo. "One thing more," he said. "Anticipating General Mitchell's tactics, when we reach the land below Eagle Pass, we'll have to stay far back on the high land, so far back that we won't know when Standish arrives. We could send out spotters, but they might be seen. The general won't come all this way to have it all blow up in his face because we're seen."

"Which means you want me to get away and tell you when Standish reaches the spot," Fargo said.

"You've got it. The general will have to attack before de los Santos has his whole force across the river," Major Nelson said, and walked outside with Fargo. "Good luck to you, Fargo," he said with a handshake as the Trailsman swung onto the Ovaro.

"Good luck to both of us," Fargo said.

The major nodded agreement, turned, and hurried to his men as they prepared to break camp.

Fargo sent the pinto through the night, racing the moon as it slid down to the corner of the sky, and he reached the flats with the night still cloaking the land. He dismounted, led the horse back to the low rocks, quickly and quietly took the saddle off, and then crept up into the rocks where he'd left his bedroll. He lay down, slept at once, and managed a few hours of rest before waking and going down to the campsite.

Jill tossed him a probing glance as she handed him a tin cup of coffee, he noted. He let the hot brew send its bracing tonic through him and he sipped it slowly.

Standish paused at his side. "I'm expecting the rest of my men today," the man said. "But we'll still have to stay here till my supplies reach us, so it's even more important you keep a sharp watch on things. You think that cavalry patrol might come back?"

Fargo let himself consider the question for a moment. "Can't rule it out, but I doubt it. I'll keep a special eye south, though," he answered, and Standish walked on with a smile of confidence. Fargo returned the cup to Jill and received another sharp, probing glance. "You still have your nose out of joint because I said no last night?" he muttered.

"We'll talk about it later," she said coolly.

Fargo walked to the pinto and began to saddle up. He'd finished when Clare came by, let her hand rest on his arm for Standish's benefit, and added a warm smile. She appeared to be flirting, certainly turning on the charm, but her words didn't match the smile. "We have to talk tonight," she said.

He returned her smile, passed one hand over the

lemon hair. "I'll get to you," he said, and she nodded almost coquettishly as she stepped back. He sent the pinto on around the perimeter of the camp.

Two wagons of new arrivals were just entering as he rode away, and he saw Standish hurrying to greet them. Once past the low rocks, Fargo turned the horse south and began to climb into the higher land, his eyes sweeping the ground for the Apache hoofprints. He found them easily enough, followed them to the uneven ridge and down the other side. A line of cottonwoods stretched across the bottom of the hill, and he slowed as he smelled the odor of hides drying in the hot sun and the unmistakable scent of fish oil.

He nosed the pinto through the cottonwoods until he heard the voices. He slid noiselessly from the saddle, crept forward till he neared the edge of the trees, from where he could see the camp beyond: a long rectangle, a full Apache camp replete with wickiups instead of the tepees used by the Plains Indians.

Fargo scanned the cluster of ponies and made a quick count of fifty; he brought his gaze back to the camp and saw some two dozen squaws, some young, and most of the braves along the far edge, relaxed, sharpening arrowheads, knives, making bows. He watched for another few minutes and then silently backed away, returned to the Ovaro, and rode from the trees. Back in open land, he slowed, halted in the shade of a tall rock, and slid to the ground.

He frowned into space. He'd had no real reason to find the Apache camp, and yet he'd had to do it. Something inside him had made him, a kind of inner voice, as though he'd had no choice. He knew the existence of a sixth sense, had seen it work often enough in man and in animal. But this had been another kind of strangeness, the kind of message a shaman experiences, a vision to make itself known when the time comes. But he was certain of one thing.

He'd not be scoffing at it. He'd seen too many unexplained things in nature and man to do that.

Slowly, the Trailsman rose and returned to the saddle and let the pinto amble along the rock-strewn land. He made a wide circle at the outer edges of the flat land, letting the day slowly slide to a close. He returned to Standish's camp as dusk sifted down. The campsite was crowded now and he saw Standish holding court at one end. He skirted the perimeter and drew to a halt where Jill warmed pieces of meat over a low fire and Clare sat nearby.

"White-tailed deer. Some of the new arrivals brought it and gave it to the number-one man, of course," Jill said.

Fargo folded himself next to Clare when he saw Standish returning. "In the center of the rocks behind us," he said quickly, and offered a welcoming smile to Standish as the man sat down.

"See anything today?" Standish asked.

"No cavalry," Fargo said between bites. "But too many Apache tracks. I don't like it."

"I still think they won't take on a force this size," Standish said.

"I'm going to ride earlier, maybe stay later, see if I can find what they're up to," Fargo said.

"Do whatever you think best," Standish said. "Been talking to the men all day, going over what's expected of them. I'm tired. I'm going to turn in early."

" 'Night," Fargo said. He finished the meal and walked to where he'd left the pinto. He took his bedroll and made his way up the low rocks, stayed on the narrow passage in the very center, and put down his bedroll when he neared the top, where he found a small hollow surrounded by flat-sided stones. He stretched out, undressed to trousers.

The night stayed warm, the stones still emanating the baked-in rays of the day's sun. He tried not to think of how little could go right and how much could go wrong, and he let his mind idle, his eyes moving from star to star in the blue velvet sky.

Almost an hour had passed when he heard the footsteps moving up the passage, tentative steps, and he tossed a handful of pebbles against the rock. The steps hurried forward and he sat up as the figure rounded the stone slab and stepped into the hollow. "Jill, dammit!" He frowned. "What are you doing here?"

"I wasn't invited, but I thought I'd come anyway," she said, her smile acid.

"It's your damn bitchy jealousy working again," he snapped.

"It's my curiosity," she said. "Where'd you go last night?"

He felt surprise stab at him as he heard Clare moving up the path. "Dammit," he muttered aloud. "Dammit!"

7

Clare stepped into the hollow and stopped, surprise flaring in her eyes as she saw Jill, then a flash of uncertainty following. "What is she doing here?" She frowned.

"Leaving," Fargo bit out.

Jill snapped a glare at him. "Why?"

"Because I said so," Fargo growled.

"Not till you answer my question. Where'd you go last night?" Jill persisted.

"I'm not answering it," he said.

"You don't trust me," Jill said, and looked injured.

"I don't trust jealous women," Fargo said. "They see through eyes that distort everything. They hear with ears that hear wrong. They think with a head that twists everything." Jill bit her lower lip and glowered at him. "Now go back and be quiet about it," he said sternly.

Jill turned, her head down and her lips tight. "She better come back down damn soon," she muttered as she passed Clare.

When Jill left the hollow, Clare came forward, her eyes searching Fargo's face. "She can be trouble. You're right about jealous women. Can you control her?" Clare asked.

"I'll see to it. She's more afraid than anything else," Fargo said, and sat down on the bedroll.

"What we do must stay between us. There's too much risk in bringing anyone else in," Clare said.

"I know," he agreed, and Clare lowered herself to the bedroll, a quick, graceful movement, her breasts pressing the blouse for an instant, twin points as delicate as the rest of her.

She offered a sidelong glance. "Where *did* you go last night?" she asked, the question suddenly all female rather than all business.

He smiled. "Tracking down the U.S. cavalry," he said, and enjoyed the surprise that flooded into her face. He quickly told her everything that had happened, and when he finished, her fingers were digging into his arm.

"Can we hope? Dare we?" she murmured.

"Hope is free for anyone," he said. "I still have to buy time. Everything depends on that."

"Maybe you can start soon," Clare said. "It's why I came tonight. I signed vouchers today to pay for eight wagons of rifles, ammunition, and gunpowder, supplies Standish is to bring to de los Santos when they meet."

"When are they due?" Fargo asked as the excitement began to spiral inside him.

"The day after tomorrow. They might be a few days later," Clare said. "They'll be coming from the west, Standish mentioned."

"If those wagons don't arrive, he'll be delayed for sure," Fargo said.

"Can you stop them, just you?"

"I don't know, but I'm sure as hell going to try," he said, rose, and pulled her to her feet. "You get back to camp, stay relaxed, play it out."

She nodded and his hands held her waist, slender warm softness. "Standish feels confident. I'll keep him that way. I'll keep resenting him. It makes him feel he has things in hand," she said, and her lips suddenly lifted, touched his, a delicate kiss that was over as quickly as it had come. "Good luck," she whispered, slipped from his hands, and hurried away.

He listened to her hurry down the rocks until he could no longer hear her; then he lay down again on the bedroll. Excitement kept sleep away as he tried to form plans only to realize he could form nothing until he saw the wagons. But a chance waited that he'd not let pass by, that much was certain, he told himself. Hope was still a thing of wishes and prayers, but perhaps he could give it some substance.

An hour had passed and he had just turned on his side to pull sleep around him when he heard the footsteps in the passage. He half-rose, the Colt in his hand as the figure stepped around the rock and into the hollow, the blue robe pulled tight around him. "Back again, dammit?" he bit out harshly.

"I'm sorry. I had to come back. I waited till everyone was asleep," Jill said.

"Everyone meaning Clare," he grunted.

"Yes," she admitted as she sank down beside him. "Are you real angry with me?" she asked, arms encircling his neck. "I'm just afraid. I don't want to be left out."

"We talked about this," he reminded her.

"I know, and I'm sorry. I'm jealous, you're right. Because I care about you. I'm afraid for both of us," she said. "I'll do better. I promise."

"See to it," he grunted, and she came against him, pressed him back to the bedroll, and lay half atop him, the robe pulled open, her breasts soft warmness against his chest.

"I'll go back before daybreak." She rubbed against him, and her lips found his, desperateness in their eager touch.

He shrugged. This night might well be the last such one until it was over.

Later, when she slept against him, satiated and satisfied, he realized she used her body as a weapon against her own jealousy, a catharsis and a reassurance. He hoped it would work, but it didn't change his mind about jealous women. He'd tell her no more than she already knew.

He slept again till morning came, and when he returned to the campsite, he found Standish preparing to put his small army through some drills, a maneuver designed more to keep the men occupied than disciplined.

"I may not be back, come dark," Fargo said to the man. "I keep seeing fresh Apache tracks and no Apache. They may be moving in by night. If so, I want to know why and how many. It'd be unusual for them."

"Do whatever you have to do," Standish said, and strode on.

Fargo exchanged a quick glance with Clare as she laid two washed blouses on a rock to dry under the sun. Jill blew him a kiss as he rode from the camp. Once behind the low rocks, he put the Ovaro into a gallop. He streaked westward, finally came to highland that let him climb up to scan the terrain ahead. He saw nothing and continued on the high land until the afternoon wore toward a close. He had climbed a long, rock ledge from where he could gaze down at the gulleys and ravines that cut through the rock ahead when he spotted the slow-moving objects, hardly more than dots in the distance. He backed from the ledge, sent the pinto scrambling through narrow passages in the high rocks, and the dots took on shape and form, became wagons. He moved closer to see they were mostly California rack beds, long and heavy with fifty-two-inch-high wheels for mountain work.

The Trailsman shot a glance at the sun and saw it begin to disappear in the horizon. The wagons would stop for the night and go on to Standish in the morning, he knew. The high rock passages were no place to drive a wagon by dark. He watched the line move slowly down a passage. Each wagon was covered by a tarpaulin tightly tied down to the top of the body frame, and he counted a driver and a helper with each wagon, sixteen men in all.

He drew closer while staying high and looked down on the line of wagons as they reached a place where the rocks widened to offer a flat table of stone. The wagons were drawn into a U shape; the horses were unhitched and taken to the other side of the table of land where a thin line of mountain grass had found soil enough to grow.

Fargo dismounted, knelt on one knee, and continued to watch as the men built a campfire and ate quickly, took their gear, and began to settle down for the night. Some slept alongside the wagons, others near one of the tall boulders at one side, and a half-dozen wrapped themselves in their blankets in the open space near the fire as night descended. They were all hard asleep in minutes.

Fargo began to move down toward the camp, the Ovaro following behind until he halted again when he was almost at the edge of the table of land. His lips pulled back in a grimace as he scanned the camp, his gaze traveling slowly across the wagons. He had to find one carrying gunpowder, but the canvas wrapping revealed nothing. He'd have to examine each one.

He left the Ovaro and moved forward, crept along the side of rock to the first wagon. Keeping the wagons between himself and the fire, he began to run his hands across the tarpaulin, pressing down to feel the shapes beneath. Long, square shapes took form under the first wagon's tarpaulin. Boxes of rifles. The next three wagons held more of the same, and he paused before the fourth one, where two men slept alongside the wheels.

The Trailsman moved forward carefully, again ran his hands along the canvas covering. More boxes, but short ones this time, stacked in long rows. Ammunition, he muttered silently, and went on to the next wagon. He pressed into the tarpaulin and halted, his fingers finding the curved sides of gunpowder casks. There were other wagons carrying gunpowder, he was certain, but he only needed one.

Fargo reached down to his ankle and drew the razor-sharp double-edged throwing knife from its holster. He threw another quick glance at the two men sleeping nearby, saw they were hard asleep, and he began to cut the ropes holding the tarpaulin down to the corner of the wagon frame. When he had the ropes cut, he could lift the canvas high enough to see the cask and pull it from the wagon. He set it carefully on the ground and used the knife again to pry the lid open. Holding the cask with both hands, he moved along the wagons and poured the gunpowder over most of them. It was a precaution, he realized. When one erupted, the others would also. Yet he wanted as much assurance as possible, and when he finished, he set the open cask on its side atop the wagon where he'd taken in.

He took the rope that had tied the tarpaulin corner to the wagon bed, used the knife to scrape it into frazzled, thin strands, and placed one end into the opened cask; he strung the rest down along the side of the wagon to the ground. He left it dangling and his eyes scanned the open space to the still-burning fire. The Colt in one hand, he dropped into a crouch and started across the open area toward the fire, stepping carefully around the first two sleep forms, skirting two more. He was almost at the fire when he heard one of the men nearby stir, and he dropped to one knee.

The man pushed up on one elbow, pulled his eyes open, blinked. He had just cleared sleep from his eyes when Fargo brought the Colt down on his head, and he fell back onto his blanket.

The Trailsman took three long, quick steps to the fire, grabbed hold of the end of one burning stick, and pulled it free. The other end burned with a small but steady flame. He forced himself to take slow, careful steps back across the camp, again skirting the figures that slept in the open ground. When he reached the wagon with the gunpowder, he paused, eyed the dangling strand he'd frazzled to burn quickly, and hoped he'd left enough time to reach the rocks where he'd left the Ovaro. He reached out with the burning end of the stick, touched the rope, waited another few seconds until he was certain it had caught fire, and then dropped the stick and raced back along the edge of the rocks.

He made no attempt at silence now. Silence was a luxury he could no longer afford, and he heard some of the men wake, half-grunt, and sit up. But he reached the rocks and flung himself into the passageway where the Ovaro waited. He halted, turned, let himself peer over the edge of the rock just in time to see the wagon of gunpowder explode with a towering sheet of flame. A series of mammoth flashes followed, and the night was filled with sudden thunder and lightning. He saw the debris of wagons hurled into the blackness, and the spread-eagled silhouettes of bodies as the ammunition and gunpowder continued to explode. Most of the horses along the far side seemed to escape being blown to pieces, and as the thunderous explosions began to subside, Fargo heard the shocked shouts and groans of those who had somehow been able to survive.

Through the smoke that covered the area he saw three figures stagger aimlessly, then a fourth, all obviously alive because they had slept at the far edge of the table of land. Fargo lowered his head, turned, and backed the Ovaro up the passage until he found a spot wide enough to circle and mount. He rode away, the acrid scent of burning gunpowder still filling his nostrils. It didn't go away until he was hours from the spot and racing east through the night.

The moon had begun to slide toward the dark horizon when he reached the flats; he rode along the edge of the encampment to where Standish slept. He spotted the last glint of the moon against the lemon-yellow hair, dismounted, unsaddled the horse, and set his bedroll down. He slept immediately to wake only when morning stirred the camp.

Fargo rose slowly, used his canteen to wash, and took a cup of coffee from Jill when he was dressed. His pleasant smile ignored the curiosity in her eyes and turned to answering Standish's questions.

"No, I didn't spot any coming by night," Fargo said. "But I covered a fair-sized stretch of land. They could've gotten past me."

"I wouldn't be concerned with the Apache," Standish said. "Just keep your eyes open for that damn cavalry patrol in case it circles back this way."

"I will. I'll be going out later. My horse pulled a pastern tendon. I want to give him a few hours' extra rest," Fargo said, and settled back as Standish walked out to where the main body of his mercenaries were just waking.

"We'll practice riding in columns of four today," he heard Standish say. "We don't want to look like a bunch of stragglers in front of the Mexicans," the man added, an appeal for personal pride edged with a touch of patriotism.

"Don't matter a damn to me," one man said, and a murmur of agreement rose from the others.

Fargo smiled wryly as Standish continued his try at keeping the men occupied.

"All right, forget about the Mexicans. A little military precision will help you fight better," Standish said.

"Fight who?" someone called out.

"Once we're established, the government will have to send whatever they can against us, and there may be some attempts at organized resistance along the border towns," Standish said. "So let's work out some."

Fargo watched as the men grumbled but took to their mounts. He was still relaxing when Clare paused beside him.

"Have a nice night?" she asked casually.

"Very nice." He smiled, and she nodded and moved away. He saw Lew Barkins and Sam White preparing to ride out, each with an extra rifle across the saddle. "Something special?" he asked.

"The boss is sending us and ten other men out to bring back some fresh meat," Barkins said.

"Lots of white-tail south," Fargo said, and Barkins nodded as he rode away. The Trailsman let another hour go by and dozed, aware of Jill's eyes on him, and when he finally rose, she came over to the Ovaro.

"Can I come visit tonight?" she asked.

"No, you stay in camp. Standish is going to be sleeping poorly tonight," he said, "I'll likely sleep in camp, too."

"How do you know he'll be sleeping poorly?" she asked at once.

"He's getting more tense every day," Fargo said, patted her cheek, and rode from the encampment. He turned the horse west when he was past the low rocks and hadn't gone more than a few miles when he spotted the handful of figures moving toward him. Two rode the half-burned and splintered remains of a wagon with only the front wheels on it, the remainder of the body dragging along the ground. The other three were on horseback.

Fargo halted when he reached them. "You boys have some trouble?" he asked.

One of the men spit at his question. "You know where a feller named Herb Standish is camped, mister?" he asked.

"I do. I'll take you to him." Fargo began to lead the way to the flats. He kept his face expressionless as he rode into the encampment with the straggling figures in his wake and saw Standish get to his feet, stare, a frown of alarm start to slide across his face. "Found these gents. They said they were looking for you," Fargo told Standish, and moved to one side and dismounted as Standish approached the men, his eyes still staring.

"Who are you?" Standish barked.

"We were with the wagons," the same man said, and slid to the ground.

Fargo watched Standish's jaw drop, his stare begin to gather a mixture of panic and fury. "The wagons? My wagons with the rifles, ammunition and gunpowder?" Standish asked. The man nodded, shrugged unhappily, and Standish leapt onto him, closed both hands around the man's throat. "What happened? Goddamn you, what happened?" he roared, and shook the man as a dog shakes a bone.

"Blew up," the man gasped out, his voice a strained rasp. "Everything blew up."

Standish, his face contorted in fury, flung the man to the ground and spun on the others. "Talk to me, goddammit. How? Why?" he shouted.

"We were camped. Everybody was sleeping," the man said. "Suddenly all hell broke loose. All we can figure is that it must've been a spark from the fire."

Standish clapped his hands to his face, half-turned away as the man struggled to his feet and his companions looked on, still in shock. "God, oh, my God," Standish wailed, pulled his hands down, and spun on the man again. "There's nothing left? Nothing?" he asked.

"We're all that's left," the man said.

"Goddamn idiots, that's what you are," Standish raged. "You get me those guns and the ammunition. I made a commitment to bring them with me."

"There's no way we can make up that shipment, Mr. Standish," the man said. "There's a trader, two days' ride from here, old Jack Jackson. Maybe we could get fifty guns from him, but no more."

Standish lashed out again, pulled the man to him, his face contorted. "Get them. Get whatever you can, goddamn you," he snarled. "Bring them back here and all the ammunition you can get. I'll hold two of your friends. You don't come back, they're dead."

"Yes, sir," the man said, backing away. "We'll come back with as much as we can," he said.

One of Standish's men trained his six-gun on two of the men, and the other three took the horses and hurried away.

"Tie them up and use what's left of that wagon for firewood," Standish bit out, whirled, and drove his fist into the palm of his hand. "Goddamn morons, building a fire near a powder wagon," he said. "This'll mean a two-day delay at least. Goddamn, can't anybody do anything right." He spun again in the dusk, stalked out among his hired hands, and lashed out in frustrated fury. "Tomorrow you're gonna get some proper riding in, or you can get out and forget the rest of your money," he said. "And I want everybody to clean his horse's hooves. I don't want any sore-footed nags slowing us down when we move."

He turned again and strode back to where Fargo lounged on the ground and Jill had a small cooking fire started. "You ride those hills tomorrow and keep a sharp eye out for any trouble, Fargo," he barked, and Fargo nodded, watched him halt in front of Clare.

"I suppose this makes you happy, bitch," he snarled, and Clare's cool expression never changed. His lips worked as he fought to find the right words to throw at her; then he saw Lew Barkins and the other men had returned and they took his attention.

"Sorry it got so late, Mr. Standish," Barkins said.

"Take it away and skin it. We'll use the meat tomorrow," Standish ordered crossly, and folded himself against one of the tall rocks.

The supper meal was taken in almost absolute silence, and the night grew still. Clare allowed Fargo to see a tiny smile touch her lips as she passed him. He took his bedroll to the rocks a few yards away but still well within the campsite. Jill dragged her bedroll near his and settled down, watched him undress and stretch out.

" 'Night," he said.

"You've got real sixth sense," Jill whispered. "Knowing that Standish would sleep poorly tonight."

"It's a gift," he muttered, turned his back on her, and slept at once. But not so soundly that he didn't enjoy hearing Standish get up and pace the ground a half-dozen times. He finally settled down and Fargo slept till the hot morning sun woke him. He dressed and watched Standish snap and snarl his way through morning coffee and stride out to the men just coming awake across the flats.

Fargo's eyes were still on Standish as he stood beside the Ovaro. "What are you thinking?" a voice said, and he turned to see Clare there. "How angry he is?" she asked.

"He's more than angry. He's nervous," Fargo said. She frowned back. "His wild dream is waiting for him, but he still has to make it happen, to put the final pieces together. All his bragging confidence is a mask. He won't stay steady under pressure."

"That's good for us," Clare said.

"No, it's bad for us," he countered, and Clare frowned again. "We need to delay him as long as we can. A steady man can take delays. A nervous one can't."

"You've done great so far. I say keep the pressure up," Clare answered.

"We've no choice." He shrugged, climbed onto the horse, and rode from the flats. Beyond the rocks, he slowly crossed and recrossed the land, noted the fresh Apache tracks that trailed over the uneven ridge, and generally wasted the day. When he returned to the encampment as dark fell, he found Standish only slightly less irritable and found himself admiring Clare's cool calmness. Toughness under delicacy. Jewelweed, he grunted.

He stayed inside the camp again as he laid out his bedroll. Jill set her blanket nearby, her glance almost smug as she undressed, let him see her naked loveliness for a brief instant, and then lay down to sleep.

When morning came, he rose early and had the Ovaro saddled before the others woke. He waited to let Standish see him ride out and spent the rest of the day in a wide circle around the flats. But he studied the surrounding terrain as he did, watching and waiting. The day had begun to fade when he returned to the camp.

Standish was pacing back and forth in front of Barkins, Clare, and Jill when he arrived. "Did you see them?" he barked as Fargo dismounted. "Those bastards who are supposed to have my rifles back today?" he followed.

"No, not a sign of anybody," Fargo said.

"Shoot the two we have," Standish snapped at Lew Barkins.

"I'd give them another day," Fargo said calmly. "Maybe two."

"Why, goddammit?" Standish exploded.

"You're not ready to move. You're still waiting. Give them some more time. You've nothing to lose by it," Fargo said.

"I might be ready to move tomorrow," Standish answered.

Fargo shrugged and turned away while the questions raced through him. He sought out Clare's eyes and found only a cool impassiveness. The deer that had been brought in the day before was distributed and served as the main course for supper. He ate slowly, relished the taste, and rose with his empty plate to hand it to Jill.

"Any more premonitions?" she asked softly.

"Not tonight," he muttered, and turned away. As he passed Clare, her voice came to him, so soft he hardly heard it.

"We must talk tonight. Same place," she said.

Fargo went on without a nod, gathered his bedroll, and walked from the camp. He climbed to the center of the rocks behind, settled down, and knew he'd have at least an hour to wait. When the second hour passed, he rose and felt himself growing nervous, but he suddenly heard the footsteps approach and Clare came into the hollow.

"He took a long time to fall asleep," she said, and he took her hand as she came to him.

"He might wake again. You'd better be quick," he said as he found himself admiring how delicately lovely she looked in the moonlight, pastel touched by silver.

"I signed vouchers for two hundred horses due tomorrow," she told him. "The extra horses are another part of what the general expects him to bring."

Fargo's eyes narrowed in thought. "Two hundred horses. A dozen wranglers with them, I'd guess," he murmured.

"They're coming from the north, Standish said. He

has the signed vouchers ready and waiting," Clare told him. "He'd be beside himself if the horses didn't arrive."

"Get out of here and let me think on it," Fargo said, and she turned, paused, brushed his cheek with her lips.

"It was lucky last time. Maybe it'll be again," she said.

"Last time was different," he said.

She turned, brought her mouth to his, held for a moment, and then slipped away.

Fargo returned to his bedroll and wondered if he'd have another visitor, but none appeared and he let himself sleep, happy that Jill was keeping her promise to contain her jealousy. He slept until the hanging hour before dawn; then he let his eyes snap open and thoughts tumble freely through his head until, as the sun broke over the hills, he sat up, felt the surge of excitement course through him. He rose, dressed, awe churning inside himself. He knew he'd never have a proper explanation for it, yet it was there, falling into place, a plan in place without having been made, an answer to a question never asked.

He walked down to the camp again realizing how much more existed than the things we can touch, see, or feel. Impatience flooded through him, but he knew he had to hold back, make sure Standish saw only the ordinary. He had coffee, listened to the man grumble and snap, and finally he climbed onto the Ovaro and silently cursed the time he'd wasted.

"Hold on, Fargo," Standish called to him. "You see a couple hundred horses being driven you bring them in. I'm waiting for them."

"Sure thing." Fargo nodded and put the pinto into a canter and disappeared beyond the rocks. Out of sight of the camp, he increased speed, sent the horse racing over the dry land, riding directly north. He wanted to reach the herd as quickly as he could, survey their route, and have enough time to do what he had to do.

But it was nearly noon when he spotted the large cloud of dust, pancake-shaped, and he slowed, turned into a high place, and watched the herd of horses move under the prodding of ten wranglers. They moved in an oblong mass, well under control. He watched the wranglers guide them toward a wide gulley that inclined downward. He peered farther ahead to see the gulley level off into wide, flat passage bordered by low slopes on both sides with ample cottonwood cover.

They'd be in the downward gulley for another hour, he guessed, and the flat passage for two more. He whirled the pinto and raced back, climbed the hills, and rode hard for the uneven ridge that lay at least an hour west. He reached it, crossed over, and went down the other side without slowing. He reined up only when he came to the narrow line of cottonwoods. He dismounted, led the way through the trees until the Apache camp came into sight.

The camp was a quiet place in the heat of the burning midafternoon sun, most of the braves half-sleeping or simply lounging near the wickiups at the far side. The squaws, as usual, were working, boiling meat in water surrounded by hot stones, stretching hides. Fargo watched a young squaw, wearing only a ragged skirt, full breasts swaying as she walked, dark-brown nipples on gold-brown skin. She was young enough to still be real pretty, he noted, and he edged closer, pulling the pinto with him.

She was passing nearby and Fargo's eyes swept the rest of the camp again. It'd take the braves at least thirty seconds to get to their ponies, perhaps a little longer if he were lucky. He gathered himself, let the young squaw come a step closer, and then he leapt from the trees, seized her around the waist, and yanked her with him as she screamed. He flung her facedown across the saddle, her full breasts bouncing; then he leapt onto the horse behind her and sent the pinto into a full gallop through the trees.

They'd think it was a coup, at first, a brave from another tribe. Of course, as soon as they caught sight of him, they'd know better and the fury would become consuming rage. He reached the end of the line of trees and raced across the ground, headed west, threw a glance behind him, and saw the first of the Apache clear the trees. He turned, raced up a steep slope he knew would slow the short-legged Apache ponies, reached the top, and raced across the flat stretch.

When Fargo glanced back again, the Apache were just clambering over the top to chase after him, and he kept on, glancing back a few minutes later to see that he had at least fifty braves in pursuit. He slowed for a moment, yanked the young squaw up, and let her slide from the saddle. He raced on as she hit the ground and rolled to one side. One of the pursuers would stop for her, but the others would continue the chase. He turned down a narrow passage between two rock sides that would again slow the Apache as they'd have to lose time by filing singly through it.

Fargo had gained another fifty yards by the time they emerged from the passage and now he raced forward, anticipation growing inside him. The wranglers should have their herd into the flat ravine by now, not more than another half-hour ahead. The Apache wanted this white man who had dared to try to seize one of their squaws, and they'd keep after him for hours. But the Apache were also opportunists. Everything had a relative value, and at the top, above all else, were good horses. It was what he counted on. A herd of fine horses, even if they only rode off with some of them, was worth far more than the pursuit of a lone, crazy white man and certainly far more than the squaw.

The Trailsman glanced back again, saw the Indians had spread out as they chased after him, but their short-legged ponies hadn't gained any ground. The flat ravine was suddenly just ahead, beyond a rise. He spurred the pinto forward, crossed the rise, and saw the huge herd moving through the ravine. He drew the Colt. This part was important, too. It had to look right to the wranglers. Some of them would be left to tell what had happened. He raised the Colt and fired into the air, at least three shots, and saw the men at the rear of the herd turn in alarm.

"Apache," he yelled as he charged forward. "Apache."

The wranglers at the head of the herd had turned now, heard his shout, and as their eyes went to the rise, they saw the Apache come into sight.

Fargo glanced back, saw the Indians pause for a moment and then charge down with renewed excitement. He had reached the herd and yelled at the wranglers. "Hit the slopes, take cover and save your damn necks," he shouted.

The men wheeled their horses and began to race for the trees that dotted both slopes bordering the ravine.

He did the same, racing the Ovaro up the nearest slope, where he leapt to the ground beneath a cottonwood. He yanked the big Sharps from the saddle, took aim, and sent one of the Apache tumbling from his pony.

Some of the wranglers didn't move fast enough and he saw them go down as the Apache split up, some moving against the horses, others racing for the wranglers. Fargo saw three more of the men fall and another topple out from beneath a tree as the Indians swept along both slopes. He let two race past him, stayed low, and then rose and fired; both men flew from their mounts at the same instant. But the horses were racing in panic now, some down ravine, some up and across the slopes, others turning to flee back the way they'd come. In moments, the ravine was a place of pandemonium, with horses racing in all directions, arrows and shots filling the air, and the Apache breaking off into smaller groups to give chase to the horses.

Fargo stayed against the tree trunk and watched the Indians pursue the horses, quickly herding a dozen under control as they moved up the opposite slope.

But they hadn't enough men to chase down more than a part of the two hundred horses, which were now racing off in all directions. Fargo rose to his feet, watching as the Apache continued to round up small groups until he estimated they had brought some fifty horses under control. Staying by the tree, he watched the Apache ride off with the fifty horses they'd rounded up, waving their arms triumphantly. The chase had brought unexpected rewards. They even had the squaw back. It would indeed be a triumphant return to camp, and Fargo waited till they had ridden from sight before he rose, returned the Sharps to the saddle holster, and stepped from the tree.

Slowly, the other figures began to move into the open, most on the opposite slope, and Fargo crossed over to them. He counted four figures as they advanced to meet him, relief still in their eyes. "You the only ones left?" he asked.

"Looks that way," one of the men said. "If it hadn't been for you, mister, we'd all be dead."

"They must've been following you for some while. I only saw them when I came over the ridge," Fargo said.

"My name's Cochrane. We were on our way to the Uvalde Flats to meet a man named Standish," the wrangler said.

"I know. I scout for him. I'll take you to him," Fargo said. He waited for the men to retrieve their horses and then slowly led the way east toward the flats. They arrived with the first gray of dusk and

Fargo saw Standish get up and come forward as he led the four men to meet him. Standish's eyes focused on the first of the men, his mouth dropping open.

"Cochrane?" he offered, the single word not quite a greeting and not quite a question.

"Yes, sir, Mr. Standish," Cochrane said nervously.

"Where are my horses?" Standish asked, alarm already curling in his voice.

"The Apache jumped us. They killed six of us, ran off with some fifty of the horses," Cochrane said.

"Where are the rest of them?" Standish questioned, his small eyes surprisingly wide.

"Run off, scattered all over. We couldn't stop them. Nobody could," Cochrane said.

Standish made a strangled noise inside his throat, stared at Cochrane as his face grew white and his lips moved soundlessly. Finally the scream burst from him. "No, Jesus, no," he shrieked, and clapped both hands to the sides of his face. "No, oh, Jesus, no," he repeated, this time shaking his head from side to side. "The Apache. The goddamn, stinkin' Apache," he said, and turned on Fargo. "I thought you were going to watch for the goddamn Apache," he snarled.

"If it wasn't for him, we'd all be dead," Cochrane interrupted. "He charged down shootin' and shoutin'. He tried to warn us. It was just too late."

"Too late? I don't want to hear about too late," Standish roared. "I want my horses."

Cochrane shrugged helplessly. "It'd take fifty men to round them up, maybe more," he said.

"I've got fifty men," Standish roared, and turned to Lew Barkins in the last light of the day. "Come morning, you take fifty men and round up those horses."

"Yes, sir," Barkins said, and he hurriedly moved away.

Standish turned to Fargo. "You go along, too, and watch for the damn Indians. Maybe this time you can get to the horses before they do instead of at the same time," he barked.

"I'll try real hard," Fargo said calmly.

"Get the damn food on," Standish flung at Jill as he stalked off to sit by himself in the dark.

Fargo climbed down from the pinto, led the horse to one side, and unsaddled the animal. When he returned to the small fire, Clare was waiting and Jill had begun to serve the food. Clare's lips curled in a private smile as he met her gaze.

"The age of miracles hasn't passed," she murmured, her voice so low only he could hear.

"We try," he said, and walked on to take a plate from Jill, who gave him a bright smile.

Standish came over to eat quickly and angrily and stalked off by himself again.

Fargo took his bedroll to the edge of the rocks again as the camp began to settle down for the night.

Jill brought her blanket nearby. "It's funny how things work out, isn't it?" she said casually.

"Such as?" he answered from his bedroll.

"Your arriving just when the Apache did."

"The world's full of coincidences."

"Isn't it?" she returned blandly.

"Go to sleep," he growled, and heard her turn on her back. Damn her sharpness, he muttered silently. He decided to prod back when the moment presented itself. He closed his eyes and welcomed sleep until the new day came, the sun quickly heating the dry land. He used his canteen to wash, dressed, and was ready to ride when Barkins came by to halt before Standish.

"Get moving," the man barked. "Fargo will show you where the attack took place. Start from there."

Barkins nodded and Fargo swung in beside him as he led the way from the encampment, the fifty riders bringing up behind. "They're unhappy," Barkins said of the men that followed. "They told me they were paid to fight, not to round up horses."

"They're probably lousy at it, too." Fargo laughed.

"Only one thing made them go along with it. Their pay contract is by the day. The more days, the more pay they get when it's over," Barkins said.

Fargo smiled to himself. It was another reason the delays were infuriating Standish. He scanned the rocky hills as they rode and finally reached the flat ravine where the attack had erupted. He didn't see a single horse and watched Barkins send the riders off in different directions in groups of five. He led one group out and Fargo stayed, climbing up the long gulley that led to the ravine. He guided the pinto higher up into a rocky mound, found a spot that let him look across the terrain below and the distant ridge that led to the Apache.

He glimpsed some of the searchers below as they chased down horses they had spotted. He finally left the high spot and moved idly downward, his gaze sweeping the land as a matter of habit. The day slowly went into afternoon, and finally, as the sun began to dip behind the distant high rocks, he started to turn back toward the flats, but paused as he saw Barkins and a dozen of the mercenaries herding some fifteen horses along. He swung in alongside them and returned to the flats before dusk descended. As they neared, he spotted others knots of riders herding more of the horses along with them.

Standish was waiting beside an old three-spring grocery wagon that had seen better days, and Fargo saw the dozen long boxes inside the flat body of the wagon. "The rifles," Standish said at the question in Fargo's eyes. "Fifty lousy rifles and a hundred rounds of ammunition, that's all they came back with," Standish spit out. "They had the nerve to ask me for money for them."

"I'd guess you said no," Fargo commented.

"I told them I'd let them leave alive," he said. "They hightailed it." He brought his eyes to Lew Barkins and the other riders who straggled into the camp, and Fargo watched the frown dig into his brow as he stared at the horses. "Thirty?" Standish barked. "Thirty lousy horses?"

"They scattered all over," Barkins said. "I'd guess it'd take another four days to find them all, except for the ones the Apache took."

An expression of horror filled Standish's face. "Another four days?" he echoed. "Jesus, no, no. We're already two days late in starting." He turned away, started to walk off, and spun around and strode back. "Tomorrow, take another fifty men and bring them all back," he ordered Barkins. "Get this batch out of my sight and tie 'em up."

Barkins moved the horses away and Fargo swung to the ground. Jill was putting the last of the venison into a large skillet. She was alone and it was as good a time as any, he decided as he stepped over to her.

"You going to have any more smart-ass remarks before you turn in tonight?" he asked.

"Doesn't look like it," she said calmly.

"What's with you?" he pressed, and she turned to him, anger in her eyes.

"What's with me is that I suspect you've had a hand in all that's going wrong to delay things," she hissed.

"Ridiculous," he protested, unwilling to let anyone else in on what he and Clare were doing, especially someone as mercurial as Jill.

"I don't think it's ridiculous," she persisted. "And I don't want delays any more than Standish does. I want this over with so's we can ride away. I want it over before you decide to forget your word and get chummy with little Clare."

"You're letting your suspicious little mind get the

best of you again," Fargo said calmly. "Things just go wrong sometimes."

"Especially when they're made to go wrong," she said tartly.

"You just keep your suspicious little mind to yourself and your anxious little ass under control till this is over," he speared sharply, and was instantly sorry he'd been so harsh. "Understand?" he finished.

"I hear you," she muttered, an answer that was less than satisfying.

Fargo turned away from her. He sat beside Clare during the meal, Standish across from him, the man's face strained. "Seems to me you have to expect some delays on an operation this big," the Trailsman put out soothingly.

"Two days already, dammit," Standish said. "The general doesn't stand for delays."

"Guess he'll have to, this time," Fargo said calmly.

Standish's answer was a string of curses as he got up and strode away.

Fargo spoke to Clare without looking at her. "The delays mean more than just that to him," he said. "It's plain that he and de los Santos have a shaky agreement, in writing or not. He has to show that he can hold up his end of things, and he's screwing up on everything."

"Thanks to you," Clare whispered. "He hasn't the rifles, ammunition, or gunpowder, and now he doesn't have the horses he's supposed to bring. No wonder he's nervous, and I love it."

"He's holding you to pay for those supplies. What happens now? Is he through with you?" Fargo asked.

"Heavens, no. He'll keep me signing vouchers for everything after they pull off their coup. They'll need more supplies, food, equipment, and the money to get it. He intends hanging on to me for a long time."

"Good," Fargo said, and drew a curious frown. "It

means you're still important to him. He won't do anything to you." He rose to his feet. "Let's see what tomorrow brings," he said, and took his bedroll to the edge of the camp, undressed, and relaxed. He could only hope he had calmed Standish down some, but he doubted it. Standish hadn't the strength to wrestle with delays. He was a man of ambition without substance. But he wouldn't be the first of that kind to reach high places, Fargo realized, and his thoughts about Standish stopped as Jill came and set her blanket down nearby and prepared to sleep. "Goodnight," he said, waited, and received no answer. "Going to sulk, now?" he asked.

She kept her back to him. "I'm controlling my anxious little ass," she snapped. "Please don't bother me."

"Good," he said, and smiled as he closed his eyes. Better sulking than prying, he murmured to himself before he fell asleep.

He slept well, woke only to hear Standish pacing, and quickly returned to sleep. When morning came, he prepared to ride out again with Lew Barkins, this time a hundred of Standish's mercenaries following. But the day was almost a carbon of the day before. The extra fifty men found precious few more horses, but then they didn't know how or where to look and they didn't try terribly hard, he was certain. When the day drew to a close and he rode back to the encampment, the others herded not more than forty-five horses with them.

Once more, in the camp, he watched Standish's panic mingle with his fury. "Forty-two horses?" Standish counted. "That makes seventy-two altogether? You bastards all blind?" he shouted.

"They scattered, Mr. Standish," Lew Barkins said. "And they keep scattering more. I figure it'll take us at least two days more to find the rest."

"Two days more," Standish echoed, his voice suddenly a hoarse sound, his small eyes barely more than slits. "Five days' delay before we start to move. No, I can't, I can't." He watched the men turn away and go back to the others, and with what seemed an effort, he brought his eyes back to Fargo. "We move, come morning," he said. "We move. No more delays. Destiny doesn't wait for delays."

Shit, Fargo muttered silently and felt his stomach knot.

8

Morning came and the knot was still in Fargo's stomach. He looked out over the encampment as the small army of mercenaries began to fall into some semblance of a riding unit. Standish moved among his hired soldiers on his horse, giving orders, positioning himself in front.

Clare rode up beside him, disdain in her quiet words. "He wrapped himself in imperiousness last night. He's still wearing it," she said.

"A banty rooster can't be an eagle," Fargo grunted.

"Did you buy enough time, Fargo?" Clare whispered.

"I wish I knew," he said grimly. "It's out of my hands now. Yours, too." He grimaced and knew again how much he detested not being in control of his own tomorrows. But this would be one of those times. Events he had set in motion, steps he'd taken, wheels he had begun turning, all out of his hands now, everything hanging out beyond his touch.

Standish's voice snapped his thoughts off. "Fargo, get out there and start riding scout and breaking trail," the man said, his voice full of new bravado. "Clare, Jill, Barkins, get up here with me."

"I'll find a place to talk again," Fargo said, and sent the Ovaro forward, slowed as he passed Jill. "Happy now? We're on our way," he said.

"Yes, dammit," she said.

"You don't give a damn that two madmen may

133

change history?" he asked. "You don't care that they can help destroy your country, maybe start another war?"

"I care about loving, being happy, living my own life. I leave the rest to soldiers and statesmen and politicians."

"Only you can't do that. You can't close out the world and what happens in it."

"Try me," she said. "I'm just waiting for the moment I ride away from all this with you."

"The right way for the right reasons, I hope," he said, and spurred the pinto into a canter. He passed Standish, who tried to sit his horse like a warrior and succeeded only in looking like a popinjay. He rode on, turned south, and by the day's end the land had grown drier and flatter, with patches of saguaro mixed in with the blackjack oak. He rode grim-lipped, his eyes sweeping the terrain. It was a kind of empty exercise. The Apache this far south wouldn't have the strength to attack Standish's force. They were mostly independent tribes, seeing to their own domains, mostly against wandering Comanche. And there'd be no cavalry to watch for, though only he knew that, so he found himself wishing he could hold back the day.

But the day came to an end and they had made good time, to his disgust. They could reach the land below Eagle Pass in a few more days. He had to wonder if it had all been a hollow attempt to stop what was impossible to stop. Had General Mitchell found enough troops to march? Or was he still trying to put together a strike force? The questions danced in Fargo's head, mocking, laughing, and he shook them away with a curse. He found a double ravine with a narrow rise between that could accommodate everyone, and when the night meal was over, he took his bedroll up on a slope dotted with blackjack oak. Clare watched him go, he noted, and he was stretched on his bedroll, the camp grown still below, when he saw her climbing toward him. He rose, let her find him.

"You had things to tell me," she said.

"When we reach the meeting spot, I have to disappear," he said. "If General Mitchell was able to make it, he'll be too far back to know when we arrive; he has to stay out of sight. I'll have to slip away and tell him Standish has arrived and General de los Santos is on his way across the river."

"What do you want me to do?" she asked without hesitation, that inner strength surfacing at once even as her pastel delicacy glowed.

"You're something special," he said. "I want you to keep Standish busy, make a fuss, do anything to keep his attention on you as long as you can."

"Just tell me when the time comes. I'll do the rest," she said. He stood up with her and she smiled, her lips brushing his again, the same, fleet touch. "Good luck. It seems to be working so far," she said, and hurried away.

Fargo lay down and slept at once, and when morning broke, he was ready to ride when the sun came over the hills.

Jill, still in her blue bathrobe, stepped out as he started past her. "More secret plans last night?" she slid at him.

"Things to talk about," he said. "When are you going to stop spying?"

She managed to look contrite for a moment. "I asked myself that last night when she came back so soon after she'd left," Jill admitted.

"That's a step in the right direction," he said, and she shrugged as he rode on.

Once again, Fargo scouted the land, found a long plateau, and led the others to it. By the day's end they were but a few miles from Eagle Pass. The end of the long plateau afforded more than enough space to encamp, and a steep slope of hackberry rose at one side.

Standish was plainly excited, aware that he was drawing closer to the moment of his ambition's fulfillment, and Fargo closed his ears to the man's prattling. Finally, Standish ended his windy rhetoric and prepared for sleep.

Fargo let the camp settle down a little more, saw Jill in her blanket, and then took his bedroll with him up the steep slope of hackberry. He found a spot a few hundred yards up the slope where the foliage parted to let the full moon shine down like a pale spotlight, and he set his bedroll out and undressed. He lay awake, going over the things that lay so close now. Even if things had gone well, it could all go wrong, he realized. General Mitchell would be able to raise a barely adequate force at best. Timing was the key now. The attack had to come with half of de los Santos' force still on the other shore or in midriver. That could only happen if Fargo reached Mitchell with the signal to attack. Victory or defeat hanging on his ability to get away. Great events often turned on little things. History proved that. Small consolation, he grunted.

He had just shaken away grim thoughts when he heard the footsteps moving up the slope, low branches being brushed aside. He rose, the Colt in his hand as he peered through the night. The full moon filtered through the foliage, suddenly caught the soft glint of lemon-yellow hair, and he called out.

Clare hurried to him and he saw she wore the white cotton nightgown as he folded himself on the bedroll. "I couldn't sleep," she said, and he saw her eyes move across his muscled nakedness.

"That all?" he asked as the moonlight caught the faint flush in her cheeks.

"No," she said in a very small voice, and lowered

herself beside him. "I've something to say. If we win, it'll be because of you."

"You did your part," he said.

"It would've been nothing without you," she said. "I want to be honest all the way, Fargo. Final times are for honesty." She leaned forward and her lips were on his, stayed, held, pressed harder, and it was he who pulled back after a moment.

"No quick butterfly kisses?" he asked.

"Not tonight," she said, and her mouth was on his again, her arms encircling his neck. Her lips pressed harder, opened for him. He felt the touch of her tongue, quick, almost frightened, drawn back at once and then pushed forward again, more slowly. She raised both arms suddenly, pulled the nightgown up, and flung it to the grass and paused. His eyes moved over her beauty. The correct word, he told himself as he took in rounded shoulders, breasts that were still modest yet gracefully shaped, a long, curved line ending in upturned cups, nipples a delicate pink on areolae of pastel red. Her skin seemed to glow in the moonlight, a faint rose tint to her; she had nicely rounded hips and a surprisingly full, deep tangled nap just below a slightly curved little belly. Full, soft-skinned legs were held together as he came forward, gently pulled her down on the bedroll with him.

"Fargo," she breathed. "Oh, God, Fargo."

His hand cupped one breast and Clare cried out in pleasure. His mouth held hers, pulling, sucking, pressing, his thumb gently caressing one delicate nipple, and she half-screamed. "Oh, God, yes . . . mmmm, mmmmm, oh good, good," she murmured, and her hand flew up, came atop his to press his palm harder against her breast, and she thrust herself upward. He half-turned, his maleness burgeoning. He brought his mouth down to first one nipple, then the other, pulled,

137

caressing with lips and tongue, feeling their tiny tips grow firmer.

Clare was crying out, a low, undulating cry that combined desire and pleasure, and as his lips drew deep of her breast, she screamed.

His hand traced a slow, simmering path down her torso, circling the tiny indentation in her abdomen before it moved over the small curved roundness of her belly. "Oh, oh . . . oh, God," she cried as his hand slid through the very thick black nap to press on the pubic mound, feel its firm softness. "Fargo," Clare cried out, half-twisting her legs away as his hand moved to the bottom of the inverted triangle. He pushed between the softness, felt the moistness of her skin, and touched the very edge of the dark chalice.

"Iiiieeee . . . oh, Fargo . . . aaaiiiii . . ." Clare screamed, and screamed again as he touched the edge of the quivering, succulent lips. Her torso lifted, offered, even as she kept her thighs firmly together, moved her legs from side to side as one.

He pushed deeper, touched the wet darkness, and heard the gasped cry of pure pleasure. The rose tint to her skin had grown deeper, infused her entire body with a glowing incandescence, and he suddenly drove his hand forward, a moment of roughness, and her instant protest turned to a cry of delight as he stroked the dark wet recesses of ecstasy. "Oh, my God, oh, oh, oooooh," she gasped. He pressed into her thighs, suddenly felt them come open and her hips thrust forward, then just as quickly fall back and her thighs close.

"No, honey," he whispered. "No." He brought his body over hers, let the throbbing warmth of his maleness fall against the tangled nap. Clare screamed again, her body twisting from side to side. He moved, let himself push into her still-closed thighs, and her legs came apart, quivering, staying apart as he brought himself to the portal, slid slowly into the tunnel.

"Oh, oh, ooooh, aaaah," Clare murmured, her hands digging into his back. "Oh, yes, yes, yeeeessss . . ." she breathed, and moved with him, slowly, sensuously, and tiny sounds of pleasure fell from her lips, her mouth opened, her arms suddenly thrown back to press down against the bedroll, every part of her trying to absorb the devouring pleasure.

He was ready, holding back his own final burst of ecstasy, when her arms suddenly lifted and clamped around his neck. She drew herself hard against him, lemon-blond hair against his cheek, the modest breasts pressed into his chest, and he felt her thighs draw up until, almost as though she were trying to become a round ball, she clung to him as her pelvis pumped with quivering fury.

"Oh, God, oh, God, oh, now, now . . . oh, God," she gasped out, each word flung from her lips with a half-shrieked rush of air. Her moistness flowed over him, softness pressing around him in tiny spasms. He exploded with her as she screamed into his shoulder. But she continued to cling, her hands dug into his back, soft thighs wrapped around his hips as she pumped again, again, and finally slowed, quivered, held trembling against him. He felt her arms grow limp first, then the smooth softness of her thighs fall away and she let herself collapse onto the bedroll, her breasts still quivering, gray eyes staring at him with a kind of disbelief.

He gazed at her, all the pastel beauty of her still there but heightened, suffused with a rose flush that gave her smooth skin a new loveliness. "Jewelweed," he murmured as he rested half over her and let his lips brush the light-pink nipples as she moaned little sounds of delight. "Almost a first time," he said, and she nodded.

"Almost," she said. "I didn't expect it would happen, not at first, and then I began to realize that it would, then that it had to happen, tonight, before it was too late." Her hands came up, clasped around his neck, and a sudden mischievousness touched her face. "Are you sorry?" she asked.

"Only that we don't have more time," he said. "You'd best get back."

"Does it matter anymore?" she asked, and sat up, modest breasts swaying in lovely unison.

"It'll matter until it's over. Standish is unpredictable. He threw you at me to get me to stay on, but now he might feel we're conspiring. He's a madman."

"He is," she agreed, and drew on the loose nightgown. "We wouldn't conspire, would we?" She laughed, a soft sound, and he rose with her. She let her lips cling to his again before she hurried away.

He returned to the bedroll, still warm with the touch of her, still sweet with the smell of her. He slept at once and woke only when the new sun replaced the moon with its own burning spotlight.

He rose, dressed, and felt the grimness come over him at once. Reality had chased away rapture. The hornet's nest still lay ahead. He walked down to the encampment and saw Standish talking to four of his mercenaries. Jill, her back to him, half-turned with a coffeecup in her hand, saw him, and looked away. "Fargo, over here," Standish called, beckoning to him. He smiled affably as Fargo approached and halted before him. "I've a new job for you," Standish said, the smile still on his lips.

"Such as?" Fargo asked.

"Wearing irons," Standish roared, the smile vanishing.

Fargo started to reach for the Colt, aware only that something had gone suddenly wrong, but the four men were atop him at once, two seizing each arm and yanking the gun from its holster. He felt his arms pulled behind him and the coldness of wrist irons snapped closed against his skin. "Traitor, not Trails-man," Standish snarled. "Bastard." He lashed out and slapped Fargo across the face with the back of his hand, his small eyes hardly more than slits, his face a dark red in fury. He stepped back a pace and Fargo saw Lew Barkins move forward with a rope tied around Clare's neck. "Yes, I know about her, too. She told you about the rifles and the horses and you did the rest, goddamn you," Standish bit out. "But there won't be any more of it. All she's going to do is sign vouch-ers and stay tied. I'd kill you right now, but I want to throw you in front of de los Santos. You'll be proof of why I'm late and without the supplies I was supposed to bring."

Fargo's eyes went to Clare and saw the pain and defeat in the gray orbs. He brought his gaze back to Standish. "How'd you find out?" he asked.

"That's my business," Standish barked, and nodded to one of the men holding Fargo. "Tie his ankles and throw him in the wagon," he ordered.

Fargo felt the lariat immediately circle his ankles; then it was pulled tight and knotted. He sought Clare again and saw she stood with her eyes on the ground. His gaze moved past Standish and found Jill. She still stood with her back to him and he felt the frown dig into his brow first, then the gathering disbelief, and finally the realization exploding inside him. He stared at her, eyes burning into her back, but she refused to turn.

"Damn you, Jill Foster," he roared. "Damn you." She didn't move, didn't turn, and he felt the man dragging him to the wagon. "Why, dammit?" he shouted at her, his neck craned. "Why?" She continued to stand with her back to him, he saw, as he was lifted and thrown into the wagon alongside the boxes of rifles.

One of the men climbed in to sit beside him while the driver took the reins.

Standish, on his horse, now, paused beside the wagon. "We'll be at the Rio Grande by tomorrow. I don't need you now, anyway. I'll let the general kill you after I tell him what you did. He enjoys killing," Standish said, and hurried on. "Forward," he shouted, and the wagon started to roll. He looked out and found Clare on her horse, Lew Barkins riding alongside her holding the other end of the rope tied around her neck.

Fargo sat back and let the churning inside him finally subside while he continued to think about Jill. Had she planned this all along? he wondered. Had she always planned to throw her lot in with Standish if he drew close enough to his goal? Or had jealousy suddenly made her snap? He shook away the questions he couldn't answer, and fought away the overwhelming feeling of helplessness. He refused to embrace defeat. It wasn't in him, not until it became a final reality, and he let himself watch Standish's army as it rode slowly but steadily south.

It was midafternoon when Standish called a halt as they came to a sluggish stream that was wide enough and long enough to offer water to horses and men.

"You're getting out," the guard inside the wagon muttered as he dropped to the ground and pulled his prisoner with him. He sat Fargo on the ground, tied him to the rear wheel of the wagon, and strode off to join the others at the stream.

Fargo cursed silently and tried pressing his wrists against the iron cuffs. He quickly realized he couldn't slip his hands free or loosen the iron bands.

He stopped trying as he felt his skin scraped raw, then he leaned back against the wagon wheel and closed his eyes. Perhaps ten minutes had passed when he felt more than heard someone standing over him;

he snapped his eyes open, stared up into the sun, and the figure took shape, soft brown hair falling almost to her shoulders. He peered at her and saw the hardness in her even-featured face. "Why?" he asked. "Why, dammit?"

"Bastard," Jill hissed. "I climbed up to come to you last night. I waited till it was late. It seems I waited too long. I could hear her before I was halfway there."

"So that's it," Fargo said.

"Yes, that's it, you bastard," she flung back. "You gave me your word."

"It just happened. It wasn't planned."

"I don't believe that," she said bitterly. "I knew it would happen sooner or later. I just kept hoping I was wrong. But I wasn't. You and little Miss Clare were going to ride off together and to hell with Jill."

"No, dammit," he said. "I never figured to leave you behind."

"I know, and you didn't plan to screw her either. You just told me that," she sneered, the bitter anger wrapping each word.

"The one has nothing to do with the other."

"It does to me," Jill snapped.

"So now I'm waiting for a bullet or a sword from a crazy Mexican general and you're happy?" he speared.

"Happy has nothing to do with it. Survival does. Cutting a deal for myself, making the best of being ditched," she returned.

"Jealousy, your goddamn jealousy, that's what it is," he told her, but he knew that was only half of it. Being afraid was the other half. Jealousy and fear— put them together and it was like putting a match to gunpowder. He drew a deep sigh and there was sadness in his voice suddenly. "I wouldn't have left you, no matter what else," he said. "You'll have to live with that the rest of your life. And when your hurt and jealousy wear away, you'll know it, deep inside yourself, where you can't ever wash it away. Now get out of my sight and leave me alone."

"To hell with you, Fargo," she said, but he heard the sob in her voice as she strode away. The guard passed her on the way back, lifted Fargo to his feet, and helped push him into the wagon.

The trek south continued and the day wore to a close. They halted and the Trailsman knew they'd reach the Rio Grande the next morning. As he was lifted from the wagon, he saw that Standish had halted in what was probably the last pocket of land with blackjack oak before the dry expanse that led to the river.

He caught a glimpse of Clare, the rope still around her neck, but now with Standish holding it. Two of the men hauled him from the wagon and pushed him down against the trunk of a young tree, circled his chest with ropes, and bound him to it.

"Let's get us something to eat," one said as they both walked off to join the others.

The night descended, blackness over the encampment until the full moon rose to scatter its pale light and outline the shapes of men and horses. Fargo listened to the camp grow still, save for the snores and heavy breathing. He tried again to pull his wrists from the irons and quickly gave up, put his head back, and half-dozed as the night wore on.

He wondered if General Mitchell had gathered enough men to make the forced ride, if he were there waiting for the dawn and the messenger that would never come. If so, he'd be like a bride waiting at the altar, suddenly realizing the groom was never coming. And like the bride, he'd have no choice but to flee. He could never face de los Santos' full force with Standish's mercenaries added.

Fargo cursed, twisted his body against the ropes, pulled his ankles, and finally fell back gasping with the frantic effort. He sat still as the frustration raged inside him, his head back against the thin tree trunk, the full moon mocking in its serenity. He had just closed his eyes, but he snapped them open again as he heard the soft footsteps coming near. The figure stepped into sight, soft brown hair touched by the moon's pale light.

"What do you want here?" he asked. "There's nothing more to say."

"Damn you, Fargo," Jill hissed. "Damn you."

He stared at her and saw her lips trembling. "You come here to curse me out one more time?" he asked. "All right, now you can go."

She dropped to her knees in front of him, reached into her skirt pocket, drew a gun out, and tossed it in his lap.

"My Colt," he gasped. "Where'd you get it?"

"Standish had it," she said.

His brow darkened with a frown as he peered at her. "Standish give it to you?" he asked warily.

"Not exactly," she said. "He had a bottle of wine he'd been saving. I convinced him he ought to celebrate on the eve of his big day. I also convinced him I'd make a wonderful mistress."

"And he bought it," Fargo said.

"I'm an actress, remember. A damn good one," she said.

"How could I forget?"

"He drank too much and passed out. That's when I took the gun," Jill said.

"What's this mean? Second thoughts?"

"It means maybe I'm a damn fool or a softy or I don't know what or why about anything anymore," she said. "I brought the keys."

"Good girl," Fargo said, and Jill beamed.

"Lift my pants leg," Fargo instructed. "There's calf holster with a knife in it. Cut these damn ropes first," he said, and waited while she followed orders. The irons were removed slowly, so as not to rattle the chains. He pushed to his feet and threw a glance at the sky. The moon neared the horizon. Dawn lay waiting to burst forth. "I'll circle around the edge of the camp. Can you get your horse and be quiet about it?" he said. She nodded, frowned back. "You'll have to come with me."

"I knew you had something planned for the last minute," she said. "I knew you had to have. Can you still do it?"

"You're going to do it," he said. "But first we have to get away from camp. I'll meet you at the north end of camp. Now move."

He watched her for a moment and then made his way into the sleeping forms, found Standish and behind him the Ovaro tethered to a bush. He freed the horse and began to make his way past the dark figures. Three hundred horses, even at rest, did a lot of snorting and pawing dirt, and no one heard him move the pinto. He reached the end of the encampment, waited, and saw Jill come toward him with her horse. "Where's Clare?" he asked.

"With the rope around her neck and Barkins holding one end of it, two more guards alongside," Jill said.

"He's not taking any chances with her," Fargo grunted. He beckoned Jill to follow him and carefully moved away from the camp. He continued walking the horse even when he could no longer see the camp until he finally swung into the saddle and Jill came alongside him.

The first gray-pink edge of dawn streaked the horizon, and he put the horse into a canter. "They'll be coming along this way, right down to the Rio Grande, where de los Santos will be on the other side, waiting to cross." The dawn took on new strength, threw its lasso of light over the land, and Fargo had no need to describe the terrain as it unfolded before her, the long, wide plateau and the higher land that sloped up from it.

He rode down the plateau as far as he dared, the border marked by the great river almost within sight, and he turned and rode up the slope to a ridge of sandstone just high enough to hide the horses. He dismounted and lay down facing the wide plateau below. From the higher land he could see the Rio Grande and across the river, flags held high and behind them, black-and-scarlet uniformed horsemen stretching farther than he could see.

"My God," Jill breathed.

He turned, pointed east. "Back there someplace there should be a regiment of United States cavalry waiting for me to tell them that Standish has reached this point," he said, and saw the astonishment flood Jill's face. "If all had gone the way it should have, I'd have sneaked away and be riding to reach them. Standish would've figured I'd gone off scouting on my own, and he'd just move to his meeting. But now, God knows what he might do. He'll probably go on as he planned, but I can't be sure. So you'll ride in my place and I'll stay here and be ready in case he gets tricky."

Jill nodded, rose, and climbed onto her horse. "You said there should be a regiment of United States cavalry. What's that mean?" she questioned, and he offered a bitter smile.

"Just what it says, honey," he answered.

"If they're not there?" she pressed.

"Keep riding. Don't come back," he said, and saw her eyes darken. "Move, honey. Ride straight and hard."

She turned the horse and immediately went into a gallop, and he watched till she was out of sight before he flattened himself behind the low sandstone. He lay prone, his eyes not across the river but on the distant plateau. As he lay under the burning sun, the minutes seemed to be hours but finally, the dark movement appeared, a formless shape first, then becoming horses, riders, closely packed. They moved slowly closer and he made out Standish in the lead and, just behind him, Clare, the rope around her neck held by Lew Barkins. The rest of his mercenaries followed, stretched out in rows of eight.

Fargo turned his head and peered back along the land behind him and saw only emptiness and felt the hardness in the pit of his stomach. But he stayed prone, watching Standish and his men continue to come closer along the plateau. His eyes went to the river and saw the movement on the other side, flags being raised higher, more troopers coming to the fore. He returned his eyes to Standish as the man came almost abreast of him, and again, he turned to stare behind at the high plains. Again, he saw only the silent emptiness and felt the curse in his throat.

Standish had come to a halt, now in plain view of those across the river. He dismounted, waved his mercenaries to the side, and reached into his saddlebag. He drew out a flag—hand-stitched, Fargo could see— and held it aloft. "I proclaim the new Republic of Texas," he shouted. "As president, I ask the aid of our friends and allies across the border." He raised the flag again and waved it furiously.

Fargo's glance went to the other side of the river in time to see the black horse and uniformed rider move out, the horse splashing into the river as the first rows of soldiers began to follow.

Fargo kept his gaze on the lead rider, watching the man cross the river and draw up on American soil, become a tall, thin figure, a long face with sunken cheekbones and a pencil-thin black mustache. Black eyes, hard as chips of ebony, flashed with imperious authority, and a thin-lipped mouth turned down at the corners, cruelty in the very line of it. He reined to a halt in front of Standish, contempt in the gaze he threw down. "The guns, ammunition, the extra horses," he barked.

"There were problems, General," Standish said. "A traitor."

"And now there are excuses," de los Santos sneered. "We'll talk about this later. First I want my men across the river." He turned and looked back at the first two columns of soldiers that followed him ashore, and the Trailsman saw the long line begin to move into the water. Fargo turned again, peered back across the emptiness, cursed, and started to look back at the scene in front of him. But his head spun around again and he felt the fire leap inside his gut. Something moved in the distance, spread out, became a bluish horizontal shape, grew larger quickly, and took form.

"Yes, damn, yes," he heard himself mutter as the shape became blue uniforms, trimmed in gold, horses racing across the ground. As he watched, he saw the galloping riders split into two sections. One turned toward the river, the other charged straight ahead.

Fargo glanced at Standish and de los Santos, saw both frown, peer upward as the thunder of racing hooves reached them. General de los Santos' troops continued to move onto Texas soil, but there were still not more than a quarter of them across the river. Fargo turned to look back at the cavalry. The racing troopers were close, not more than a minute away; the other column reached the edge of the river, halted, and raised their carbines.

Their first fusillade sounded like a roll of thunder across the flat land and Fargo shouted in glee at the alarm on the general's thin face as he wheeled his horse and barked orders to his men.

De los Santos turned back to Standish. "What is this?" he shouted. "What have you done?"

"Nothing," Standish said, his face suddenly chalk-white. "I don't know what this is. I don't know."

Fargo rose, leapt onto the Ovaro as he saw the straight figure in the forefront of the charging cavalry regiment, wisps of white hair sticking out from beneath his uniform cap. "About time you got here, General," he said.

"Major Nelson is leading the other column," General Mitchell shouted as Fargo swung in beside him. "He'll lay down a fire that'll turn the Rio Grande red. Men can't fight in the middle of a river."

"You going straight at them?" Fargo asked as he charged forward beside Mitchell. "Standish has three hundred mercenaries with him."

"None of whom has ever met a cavalry charge," General Mitchell said. "They'll break under the concentrated fire of a disciplined attack."

Fargo saw Mitchell raise his arm into the air as they reached the sandstone ridge, glanced back to see the troopers raise their carbines into firing position as they charged without breaking stride. He shrugged, drew the Colt, and went over the edge with Mitchell beside him and saw the troopers racing up to flank them both.

Fargo fired into the crowd of mercenaries as they fell back, began to kneel, and return fire, and he saw three go down. The charging troopers alongside him split into two groups and those split into two more groups, and as they reached the flat land, they converged to set up almost a cross fire. Fargo saw Standish's men go down and saw the troopers on the other side had executed the same maneuver. They charged without a stop, fusillades crossing one another to send Standish's men falling like wheat in the wind.

The Trailsman reined up, leapt to the ground, and

reloaded as he dropped to one knee, his eyes sweeping the confusion of racing horses and running men, searching for a flash of lemon-yellow hair. He glimpsed de los Santos, flanked by ten of his men, racing for the river. He saw Standish rolling on the ground to avoid a hail of bullets that sent the dry dirt flying into the air. But no lemon-yellow hair. He cursed and caught a glimpse of Lew Barkins running in a crouch, firing back as best he could between dodging rifle fire.

"Barkins," Fargo yelled. "Where is she?"

Barkins spun, his gun raised, but he didn't fire as he saw Fargo's Colt trained on him. "She rolled under the wagon," he said, waited, and Fargo lowered the Colt. Barkins swallowed, nodded, and raced away in his crouching run.

Fargo, on one knee, spun, saw Standish's men falling back, those not dead on the ground, starting to run, spurring their horses into a gallop. He threw a glance back at the river where Major Nelson's column continued to pour fire at the few Mexican troops still in midstream. On the opposite shore, the remainder of the Mexican troops were drawing back, plainly unwilling to try to cross the river.

Fargo turned again, peered through the haze of gunsmoke, and finally found the wagon some twenty yards away.

Staying low, he ran for it, dodging bullets that smashed into the ground only inches from his feet. Some of the mercenaries were still fighting, unable or unwilling to try to run. Fargo spotted one of them raise his rifle and aim at him. He dived, twisted sideways, and the shot passed his hips by an inch. He hit the ground, rolled, came up firing, and the man shuddered, took a step forward as the rifle fell from his hands and toppled facedown.

Fargo spun and made for the wagon again and caught

the flash of lemon-yellow hair, her body hunched up between the two front wheels of the wagon.

He dropped down, reached in under the wagon, and she looked up, gray eyes wide with fear. She blinked, gasped, and fell forward into his arms. "Oh, God," she breathed as he pulled her from under the wagon. She still had the rope around her neck. He stayed low, bullets still whistling wildly past. He steered her around the front of the wagon, past the horses, and started for the edge of the plateau, where a line of rocks afforded shelter. The strangulated scream stopped him, half-anguish, half-rage.

"Fargo," the voice cried out. "You bastard, Fargo." He spun, saw Standish, a crease of red along his temple, the rifle pointed at him. "You first, then her," Standish screamed, and Fargo saw his finger tighten on the trigger.

Fargo spun, slammed into Clare, and sent her sprawling as the rifle shot exploded. He felt the bullet tear through his shirt as he twisted, hit the ground, and rolled. He came up on one knee as Standish swung the gun to Clare. Fargo brought the Colt up, fired, and heard the click of an empty hammer.

"Standish," he shouted as he charged, powerful leg muscles driving him forward. "Standish," he screamed again, saw the man hesitate, half-turn, swing the rifle directly at him. Fargo kept charging, flung himself into a forward dive as Standish fired. He felt the bullet pass through his hair.

"Bastard, stinkin' bastard," Standish shouted as he tried to lower the rifle to fire again, but Fargo crashed into his legs and he staggered backward, fell to one knee, and from almost a prone position, Fargo drove a looping blow into the man's belly.

Standish grunted, toppled onto his back, but held on to the rifle, trying again to bring it around to fire. He managed to pull the trigger just as Fargo knocked the weapon aside and felt the shot blast by his head. He seized the rifle with both hands, twisted, and the gun ripped from Standish's hands. Fargo brought it around in a short arc as Standish started to scuttle backward, smashed it down onto the man's head with all his strength. He felt the heavy stock smash deep into the man's skull, and Standish quivered, his head spouting blood. He toppled sideways stiffly and lay still and Fargo flung the rifle aside. Only when he rose did he see that Standish lay over one corner of the flag he had so triumphantly waved only minutes before.

"The president of the new Republic of Texas just resigned," Fargo muttered. "The hard way." He turned away and Clare came into his arms and he suddenly noticed the gunfire had stopped. His eyes swept the plateau. General Mitchell was riding toward him, moving through the litter of slain mercenaries. Some of his cavalrymen were at the far end of the plateau as they broke off pursuit of a band of fleeing riders.

"It's over," General Mitchell said, reining to a halt, and both he and Fargo watched Major Nelson riding up with his column behind him. Fargo's glance flicked across the river where he saw the last of the Mexican force racing away. "What happened to de los Santos?" General Mitchell asked.

"He got away, sir," the major said. "He went into the river but was smart enough not to try to cross back. He rode upriver while we were cutting down his troops."

"Doesn't much matter," General Mitchell said. "Their great plans are gone. Those things are never put back together. Some other schemers may come up with their own someday, but this one is finished." He paused, brought his gaze to the big man with the lake-blue eyes. "The country owes you, Fargo, but I wouldn't wait for any medals. This was close. It could've worked.

It could've changed history. But the close ones never make the history books."

"Didn't expect any medals, don't now," Fargo said. "What about the girl I sent? Where is she?"

General Mitchell nodded to the sandstone ridge and Fargo looked up to see Jill sitting quietly on her horse. "I told her to follow but stay back," Mitchell said, and Fargo pulled himself onto the Ovaro.

"Wait here," he said to Clare, and she nodded.

Major Nelson and the general rode up the slope with him to where Jill waited.

"We owe you, too, young lady," the general said. "You took over a key role."

She shrugged, half-smiled, but her eyes were on Fargo. He held her gaze as he spoke to the general. "Jill needs an escort to a place to get a stage going back East," he said.

"We'll take care of that," the major said.

"She also needs travel money," Fargo said, his eyes still on Jill.

"We can take care of that, too. I've a standing fund to help those who help us," Mitchell said.

Jill half-shrugged again, her eyes on Fargo. "It seems I'm all set, then," she said, a wry smile coming to her lips for an instant. She quickly wiped it away and her eyes took on boldness. "I'm not sorry about anything," she said to him.

"I'm not either, not now," he said, and her lips tightened for an instant.

She spurred her horse forward, came alongside him, and leaned over, her kiss quick yet full. "Watch for my name in the papers," she said.

"I will," he said, and turned the pinto in a circle. Jill moved away with Major Nelson, he saw, and he paused beside General Mitchell. "How many men did you bring?" he asked.

"Six hundred," the general said. "Every last man I

could find. The timing made it work. The exact right moment, the exact right place. That's what counts."

"In everything," Fargo said. He waved and sent the pinto down the slope to where Clare waited. She had taken the rope from around her neck and found her horse. He reined to a halt. "Let's go," he said.

"Where?" she asked.

"To get your mother," he said, and saw her eyes grow wide. "You had me promise to do something for you when this was over. That was it, wasn't it?" he said, and her eyes stayed wide.

"You knew all along. How?" she breathed.

"A one-eyed gopher could see that," he grunted. "Let's ride." She quickly climbed onto her horse and he led the way past the cavalry troops, now mostly dismounted for the grim business of identifying and burying the dead. "You know de los Santos got away," he said as they crossed the Rio Grande.

She grimaced. "That means he'll be at the house," she said. "It's about a two-day ride from here."

"What about his men? He has half of them left," Fargo asked.

"He'll keep some with him. He always did, sort of a personal palace guard," Clare said. "He'll send the rest back to their units or let them go their ways."

"You can tell me more about the house tonight. Let's make time now," he said as they rode from the river onto Mexican soil. He set a fast pace, and when night came, they found a soft bed of moss beside a stand of tall verbena. Clare described the house in detail, and when she was finished, she came to him with hunger, all the delicate, pastel beauty of her wanting, caressing, demanding, screaming in ecstasy until finally she lay spent, breath coming in short gasps, and he marveled again at the very undelicate passion that lay inside her. She came against him, slept at once as he settled down beside her, and they were riding again soon after the hot sun broke across the land.

A stand of wild plum afforded breakfast and Clare took him through a tiny town—not more than four sun-baked, limestone houses—where they halted for tortillas and tequila.

The day had begun to draw into dusk when she halted on a low hillock. He saw the house below—arched entranceways, terraces, balconies—just as she'd described it. He also saw a dozen uniformed guards at the front and sides of the house; he dismounted and waited for the night to descend. When it did, a string of lamps went on along the walls and arches at the front of the house, and he saw the lights go on inside at least two rooms.

"The general will be in the living room, starting to finish off a bottle of pulque," Clare said. "He'll insist Mother stay there with him. She will until he's ready to pass out, but that can be hours."

Fargo's glance went to a stable and barracks a dozen yards back from the house. "I'd guess there's another twenty men there," he muttered. "We've got to find a way to get in and out quietly. Any noise and we'll have had it."

"The living room has foot-thick walls. You can't hear anything that goes on inside it," Clare said.

"You'd hear shots." Fargo grimaced and his hand touched the Colt. He had reloaded after he'd finished off Standish, but the gun would do him no good now. Not to get to de los Santos, he grunted. "I can get in at the rear of the house, I'm sure," he said. "I see a stone staircase to a terrace."

"There's always a guard there," Clare said.

"I'll take care of him," Fargo said. "What we need is for de los Santos to be distracted so he won't hear me until I get into the living room. That's what you're going to do. You'll ride in alone and go into the living room. The general will be surprised as hell to see you. Mad as hell, too, I'm sure."

"Will he ever," Clare said. "But he'll be busy asking me a thousand questions, cursing and ranting and throwing things."

"Keep him that way," Fargo said. "Now, go on, ride in, slow and casual. Tell him you got away during the battle and came home."

She leaned over, kissed him, lingered a moment more, and then moved down from the hillock.

Fargo watched her slowly approach the house, saw two of the guards come out to meet her, step back, and watch as she went into the inner courtyard and dismounted. He waited till she disappeared into the house before he sent the pinto to the right, circled, and came up at the rear of the house. He drew as close as he dared, saw a row of high hedges almost at the rear wall, and secured the horse behind them.

The guard paced slowly at the top of the stone steps, moving along the terrace wall. Fargo darted forward, flattened himself against the side of the steps. He heard the man's footsteps move closer, pause, then begin to recede as the guard walked to the other end of the terrace.

He whirled, leapt, took the steps three at a time, and threw himself flat on the top step as he saw the guard start back from the other end of the terrace. He stayed, not daring to breathe as the man moved almost to the edge of the steps. But the guard's eyes focused out past the steps and then he turned again, started back to the other end of the terrace.

Fargo's hand closed around the double-edged throwing knife in the calf holster. He pulled it free and rose to one knee before he crept around the corner of the top step. The guard was at the far end of the terrace, turning, starting to pace his way back. Fargo let him come a few steps closer before he sprang up and saw the surprise flood the man's face.

The guard reached for the pistol at his side, but the thin throwing knife was already hurtling through the air. The man saw the blade at the last minute, the pistol only half out of his belt. He tried to twist away, but the knife hurtled into the side of his neck. He staggered sideways, his breath a suddenly gargled sound, and he reached one hand up to the knife, touched the hilt of the blade, tried to close fingers around it.

But it was a last futile gesture and it wouldn't have made any difference if he had managed to pull the knife out, Fargo knew. He rushed forward, reached the guard just as the man sank to his knees, uttered a last rasping sound, and fell onto his side. Fargo pulled the blade free and wiped it clean on the man's shirt, turned under an archway, and entered the house. He paused to put the blade back into the calf holster, then moved on silent steps along a corrior. He heard the voices from the living room, de los Santos shouting in fury.

"She's not telling me everything," Fargo heard the man shout. "I'll have her horsewhipped in the morning."

"I'm sure she's told you everything she knows, Victor," a woman answered, and Fargo smiled as he heard Clare's voice cut in.

"Go to hell, Victor," she said. "You're finished."

"*Puta,*" de los Santos screamed, and Fargo imagined him lunging for Clare. A chair overturned and he heard the man curse. Clare's laugh echoed over his oaths. The door was open a fraction and Fargo reached it, pulled it open, and slipped into the room, pulled the heavy door closed behind him. He took in a huge room, richly furnished with leather chairs and sofa, heavy pillows scattered around, drapes and tapestries on the wall. Clare's mother saw him first and her eyes widened. She was Clare in gray, he smiled inwardly, a

pastel delicacy still there but made more of a mono-
tone with worry and age, the lemon-yellow hair a
light, almost silver gray.

The general saw the woman's eyes widen and he
spun, focused on Fargo, and his thin mouth became
thinner. "Who are you?" he hissed.

"Clare sent for me," Fargo said, and de los Santos
stared at him.

"You are the one," he muttered. "The traitor Standish spoke of."

"In person," Fargo said. "I'm the one who wrecked
your big plans, smashed them into little pieces."

De los Santos let out a roar, a bull-like sound, and
spun, reached to the wall nearest him, and pulled
down a saber. He charged and Fargo stepped around a
chair to get more space. The man followed, moving
closer, the saber raised in one hand. He leapt, swung,
and Fargo ducked the blow.

"Too much pulque?" the Trailsman said as he circled, and the general roared, swung again and came
closer as Fargo pulled back. The saber was both heavy
and sharp. One direct blow from it and the fight would
be over, Fargo realized. But if he used the Colt, the
guards outside would be storming into the room in
seconds. He'd win the battle and lose the war, and
that never helped much.

De los Santos came in again and Fargo circled the
leather sofa, glimpsing Clare's mother where she'd
flattened herself against one wall. Clare was circling
behind de los Santos, he saw, but he brought his
attention back to the general as the man sent the saber
whistling through the air in a flat arc. Fargo ducked
away easily enough, but the man surprised him by
leaping onto the sofa, reaching out, and slashing with
the weapon. This time Fargo felt the blade graze his
shoulder.

With surprising lightness, de los Santos leapt over

159

the back of the sofa, landed on the balls of his feet, and began a series of sharp, straight thrusts with the saber. Fargo went backward, the only thing he could do, found some space again, and as the general thrust once more, he pulled away, tried to counter with a left, but the blow fell far short of its target.

De los Santos grew bolder, slashing right and left. Fargo felt the beads of perspiration on his forehead as he was kept ducking, back-pedaling, twisting away. The man's pulque was wearing off in fury and battle, his blows growing sharper, closer. Fargo circled again when de los Santos charged, but this time the general used the saber to thrust first, then slice, and then bring it down hard. Fargo pulled away, felt himself stumble and go down as his foot caught on one of the big pillows on the floor.

He fell against one of the stuffed chairs, managed to twist away as the general brought the saber down in a crashing blow. The weapon smashed almost all the way through the chair and caught for a moment, embedded in the springs and the stuffing. As de los Santos fought to pull it free, Fargo spun, palms on the floor, and brought a kick up that smashed into the man's ribs. De los Santos grunted in pain, staggered sideways, losing his grip on the saber. Fargo leapt to his feet. The general tried for the still-embedded saber again instead of defending himself, got his hands on the hilt of the sword as Fargo's left smashed into the side of his jaw. He staggered again, lost his grip on the weapon, and Fargo's right crashed into his face.

De los Santos went down heavily, blood pouring from a cut cheekbone. Fargo turned, grabbed at the saber as the man got to his feet. He yanked at the blade, felt it come free, and turned just in time to see de los Santos' long, thin form bearing down on him with a vase held in both hands to crash down on his head.

Fargo flung himself sideways as he let go of the saber, but the general couldn't stop his charge. He fell forward, brought the vase down, and hurled himself onto the point of the saber, which was still sticking straight up.

Fargo winced as he saw the tip of the blade come out of the man's back. De los Santos' guttural cry was drowned out by the crash of the vase against the floor. The Trailsman rose to his feet, stared at the long, thin form that lay in front of him, forehead touching the floor, midsection upraised by the hilt of the sword so that he looked like a penitent prostrating himself before an altar.

"Oh, dear God," Clare's mother said.

Fargo rose and saw Clare beside the woman, one arm around her shoulders. "Get enough things to travel with," he said. "Each of you take a sack. I'm figuring the guards won't stop you if you ride out together."

"They won't," Clare said. "We often ride together. Sometimes under the moon. I'll get Mother's horse, too."

"No running. Everything slow, casual," Fargo said.

"What will you do?" Clare asked.

"Stay here for now, lock every door from the inside, and slip out one of the windows. The guards might come looking in a few hours, maybe to get orders from the general. It'll take them another hour to get in and figure out what happened. We'll be long gone by then," Fargo said. "I'll meet you behind the hillock."

Clare nodded and left with her mother while he proceeded to lock the four doors that led into the big room. He waited then, allowed time for the two women to gather things and leave. When he was ready, he slipped out a window, closed it behind him, and hurried down the rear steps to the hedge and the Ovaro.

Clare and her mother were waiting behind the hillock when he reached them.

"Where to?" he asked.

"Across the border," Clare said. "Mother has friends she's stayed in touch with over the years, just north of Eagle Pass. They'll put us up until I can get some of the funds from the bank."

"The same funds Standish was going to use to bank-roll his new Texas?" Fargo asked.

"The very same." She smiled. "What are you going to do?" she asked as they rode through the night, her mother a few paces behind.

"Head north, maybe east some. Thought I might take in a play or two, if I can find the right actress," he said blandly.

"The hell you will," she said very undelicately. "We'll reach Mother's friends by tomorrow. The rest of the time can be ours."

"Sounds good." He smiled.

"It will be," she said.

He nodded and smiled inwardly. He'd take sheets coming off over curtains going up anytime.

LOOKING FORWARD!
The following is the opening
section from the next novel in the exciting
Trailsman series from Signet:

THE TRAILSMAN #94
DESPERATE DISPATCH

Early summer, 1860, in St. Joseph, Missouri,
where the Pony Express has just
begun—and men are already dying
to get the messages . . . .

As the shadows lengthened and a bit of welcome
evening coolness invaded the stifling and humid afternoon air, the tall man halted his big pinto stallion.
Before dismounting, he mopped at his sweaty, dust-
streaked brow with the greasy right arm of his buck-
skin shirt. Instantly he regretted the action. His nose
wrinkled in disgust as he shook his shoulder-length
black hair. That just meant his nose was assaulted by
yet another collection of repulsive odors, mostly stale
and all rank.

Broad-shouldered but whipcord lean, Skye Fargo
assured his Ovaro, whose nostrils flared in dismay

whenever Fargo got close, that they'd all feel a lot better within the hour. He tied the reins to the hitch rail that stretched in front of a two-story stone building just off the main street of St. Joseph, Missouri.

The gaudy sign over the door said it was the Alhambra Royal Turkish Bathhouse, Strictly Modern in All Respects, Cleansing Waters of Sparkling Purity, Heated by Steam. That was exactly the place the Trailsman desperately needed to visit after a month of persuading a dozen mule-drawn wagons to cross the Great Plains.

The men who owned that shipment had been in a hurry. Up in Blackhawk, a mining camp six hundred miles away in the westernmost mountains of Kansas Territory, the deepening mines had encountered a new kind of ore. Its gold was so bound in with other minerals that the usual ground-shaking stamp mills couldn't extract the precious metal. The way the mine owners explained it, they needed to ship ten tons of their confusing rock to Swansea just as fast as humanly possible, before they went broke.

Swansea was a world-renowned smelting center, with high-powered experts who could find a refining process for that refractory ore. Swansea was also across the ocean, in Wales, but they hadn't expected Fargo to take their shipment that far. Just to Missouri to get it eastbound on the Hannibal & St. Joseph Railroad, fast, and damn the expense.

The Trailsman liked jobs like that, but pushing that hard meant there had hardly been time to eat, let alone pause for anything as frivolous as a real bath. He was sure that even the stinking mules smelled better than he did, since they at least got curried every night.

A reeking puff of dust arose from Fargo's shirt

pocket when he patted it, then looked down to be sure he was still carrying the bill of lading from the St. Joe station agent, written confirmation that he had done the job. When he turned that in at the bank, a draft would be waiting, which he could cash. Then he'd have to visit the saloons and whorehouses to find his trail crew and pay them off. He'd probably have to go by the jail and bail a few of them out, too.

Earlier today, the damn railroad agent had taken half of forever to handle a half-hour job. By the time the consignment got shoveled into a gondola car and the paperwork got filled out, three o'clock had come and gone, so the bank was closed until tomorrow. That may have been just as well. Fargo knew he had no business appearing in public until he had a bath and some clean clothes.

From his saddlebag, he pulled out the paper-wrapped parcel he had just purchased from the pimply-faced clerk who had obviously been more than eager to hurry the reeking Trailsman out of his nice, clean store. But Fargo's money had been good for a new hickory shirt, a stiff pair of Levi's, new balbriggans, and the luxury of clean, dry socks.

When the Trailsman turned and started around the hitch rail, he saw a woman strolling on the boardwalk, twirling a parasol as she came his way. Even though the afternoon was getting on, it was a little early for her kind to be on the street. His mind was still set on a bath, but Fargo didn't mind a momentary distraction to enjoy the scenery.

Her crimson hat, with the shine of satin, had to be the latest style from back East, since it was something Fargo had never seen before. Most ladies' hats these days were small, just covering the crown of the head. Hers was like that, except it had a stiff appendage on the back that went out for a few inches, then dropped for about a foot, thus sheltering a profusion of golden curls that cascaded rearward.

Despite the small size of the crown, her hat sported more feathers than a Cheyenne war bonnet, though hers were egret, not eagle, and were all bunched up and tied together with silk. Expertly applied black kohl made her darting blue eyes look bigger than they were, and she had a sort of wholesome apple-cheeked look, although Fargo knew rouge when he saw it.

He also knew expensive goods when he saw them. Her beribboned saffron taffeta dress boasted a neckline that was far too low for any respectable woman. The twirling parasol kept the potent sunshine off the creamy skin of her well-rounded and prominent breasts, exposed almost down to the nipples. But the parasol didn't do a thing to stop Fargo's eager eyes from savoring the pleasant sight. Not only was it enjoyable to watch her breathe, she sauntered in such a way that her long skirts kept flouncing up to reveal well-turned ankle above her slipperlike shoes.

"At least twenty dollars a night," Fargo muttered to himself as he recalled his mission and began to turn toward the plank door of the Alhambra. He told his rising desire to simmer down, since he wasn't going to have any double-eagles to spend on an end-of-the-trail celebration until he got to the bank tomorrow.

"Good afternoon, sir," the woman greeted, her voice low and throaty. "Are you new in town?"

Momentarily nonplussed by her brazenness, Fargo just nodded. He could detect her lilac cologne. Maybe that explained why she was approaching him. She was upwind, and still ten feet away. She just hadn't got close enough to get a whiff of an unwashed Trailsman who had maybe two dollars in his pockets.

She stepped closer and got wind of him. He could tell by how she momentarily wrinkled her petite, up-turned nose. That should have ended this encounter, but she continued to sashay forward, her eyes scanning him from muck-caked boots to smoke-streaked hat. (The only way you could start a buffalo-chip fire was by fanning furiously, and Fargo's wide-brimmed, beaver-felt hat was generally the most convenient fan.)

"Did you just arrive from California?"

Fargo hadn't noticed before just how long her eyelashes were, but he couldn't miss them now, the way they batted like frolicking butterflies.

"Rocky Mountains," he grunted as he shifted his parcel of new clothes from his right arm to his left, so he'd have an easier time pushing the Alhambra's door open as soon as this high-class harlot gave up on him.

"Oh, really." She brightened. "Would you like to tell me about your journey?" Her neck twisted as she scanned the street, which was pretty much empty. Nobody was within fifty yards on this lazy summer afternoon; even over on the main street, a block away, hardly any traffic disturbed the dust. Her eager gaze returned to the Trailsman. "I have a room nearby where we could talk. You could relax with a drink."

Her sultry tone made it clear that Fargo could expect considerably more than conversation and a shot of whiskey. But this wasn't adding up right. Fargo had been accosted on the streets often, sometimes even in broad daylight. The women who solicited directly were usually missing teeth, overly plump, scar-faced, or just too old to work in the classier parlor houses.

The exquisite creature before Fargo could have been the star attraction at any high-toned bordello this side of San Francisco. Yet she was throwing herself at what had to be the grimiest man in town. Fargo felt leery of any woman who'd even consider bedding him in his current state; it was kind of sickening to think of what else she might have taken in if she was willing to take Fargo now.

"Honey," he explained, "as you've doubtlessly noticed, I need a bath worse than I need anything else right now. So let me tend to that, and if we run across each other later, we can figure out something then. I'm sure we'd both enjoy it more."

"Oh, I have a brand-new galvanized tub at my place," she chirped. "And I could make sure you got good and clean all over." She regarded him again, as if to make sure he fit a description she was carrying in her pretty little head, before lifting her gloved right hand. "My name is Penelope. You can call me Penny if you'd like. And your name is?"

Fargo doubted like hell that she'd been christened Penelope at her birth about twenty years ago, so he didn't feel any qualms about plucking a name from the air. Besides, he'd prefer that while he was in town, his name was connected to someone a lot cleaner than he was at the moment. He clasped her right hand with his and left some appalling smudges on her delicate lace-trimmed white cotton glove.

"Jethro." He smiled. "Jethro Hoon." He gazed into her darkening eyes as her face fell. "Know where there's any work to be found hereabouts? I can bust mules, swamp saloons, stoke boilers, shovel stalls, just about any old thing that needs to be done."

Her exasperated sigh interrupted Fargo. To see what would come of it, he didn't finish turning toward the door.

"But . . . but . . ." she spluttered.

"But what?"

"But you look so much like him."

"Like who?"

"Hasn't anyone ever told you how much you look like Skye Fargo, the Trailsman?"

What the hell was going on here? Penelope looked to be about as short on brains as she was long in other departments, so somebody had put her up to this. For all Fargo knew, there could be an accomplice as well as the offered tub and implied bed waiting for him in Penelope's room. Any other time, it might have been interesting to go find out. But he was tired and dirty, so he stuck with being Jethro.

He shrugged. "Mayhaps. Don't recollect exactly. Anybody ever tell you how much you look like Delilah, honey?"

He had no idea how she responded to that, because he almost jumped to the bathhouse door and got it slammed behind him a moment later. He looked for a bar or chain latch, just to be sure that he and Penelope had parted company, but through the small window, he could see her lift her skirts and traipse away.

The pasty-faced clerk stirred himself, yawned, and got to the counter. As hot and muggy as it was in here, it was no wonder the clerk acted slothful. But his surprisingly baritone voice could sure move at a fair clip.

"What will it be, sir? We have authentic Turkish luxury baths, an exact replica of those used by Sultan Yusuf the First at the original Alhambra castle, which offer the discerning bather a luxurious warm room, an elegant hot room, and a palatial steam room, for the ultimate in personal sanitation. Why, it even cleanses the very depths of your pores, so that your skin can breathe. Many people are not aware, and you may be among those unfortunates, that clogged pores often result in neurasthenia, consumption and other pulmonary disorders, neuralgia, dyspepsia, female complaints—"

Fargo interrupted the practiced presentation. "Just a plain old bath in a plain old tub, if you offer such. If not, point me to somewhere that does."

"Why, certainly, sir. Always glad to oblige a customer, we are. But I feel compelled to inform you that we have no 'plain old' tubs. Certainly ours follow the hallowed tradition—none of that newfangled galvanized iron here—but our supremely comfortable individual bathing basins are constructed of none but the stoutest, quartersawn white oak from the great hardwood forests of Michigan. Master coopers assemble these—"

"Look," Fargo interjected again, "I just want some hot water to sit in, and some soap."

Before the clerk could do much more than get started about how their pure shining-white soap was made of nothing but the exquisitely rendered tallow of fatted Cincinnati hogs and the ashes of select hardwoods, Fargo interrupted again, and this time, even in the dim, shadowy interior, the clerk could see the menace in his eyes.

"Excuse me, sir. A plain bath. That would be ten cents, payable in advance."

Fargo felt heartened that a bath was so reasonable, even in a place this fancy. He began to fish for a dime. The clerk went on.

"Soap, of course, will be an extra nickel. One of our special soft towels will be an additional five cents." Fargo continued to dig for change as the total mounted —three cents for a washcloth, another five for a back brush, an extra dime for a change of water, which, as filthy as he was, he'd certainly need; likely he'd be able to sell his first tub as a barrel of ink to a printing shop. But the total was still considerably less than the whole dollar they charged for the full Turkish bath.

He paid. The clerk excused himself and stepped out into the hall, where he hollered to an upstairs helper to get stall number four ready. When the clerk returned, he had the towel, washcloth, soap, and brush.

"It will take a few moments for our staff to draw your bath upstairs, sir," the clerk explained. "If you wish, you may relax on a chair." He gestured toward a row of straight-backed wooden chairs that looked about as comfortable as sitting on a hot stove.

Fargo had the feeling that his buckskins were so stiff that sitting down would be too much work, anyway, so he declined. "This is a pretty fancy place, for no more business than you're getting," he commented.

"Oh, we do all right," the clerk responded. "Sure, we'd get a lot more trade if we were down by the river, where all the teamsters and freighters would come in. But there are already three bathhouses down there. Where we are, we get a better sort of trade, and they're willing to pay better, too. It's hard to get more than a nickel in that part of town."

"But hell," Fargo protested, "as nearly as I can tell, you've done all of thirty-eight cents so far today. That's no way to stay in business."

"In the evening, when men want to freshen up for a night on the town, it'll pick up plenty. And on Saturdays, we're packed from morning till nigh midnight. Get a big wagon train in, and we'll be busy like that on any old day, soon as those cheap bathhouses fill up."

If he had more to say, it wasn't important. Some thumps from upstairs signaled that the Trailsman's long-awaited bath was ready.

Fargo had not stopped at the Alhambra because it was supposed to be so luxurious; he didn't care. It was just that after racing across town only to arrive at the bank about ten minutes too late, he turned to the closest spot for a bath, and the Alhambra was just right down the street.

But the place was pretty nice. The walls of the stall were whitewashed wood, not just canvas like in the cheap places. There were hooks for his clothes, a pewter pitcher for washing his hair, a chair for comfort before and after, and he'd drunk a lot of water that wasn't nearly as clean as what was steaming in the tub.

Eagerly he sat down, tugged off his boots and socks, then laid his new clothes on the chair, atop his Colt and the thin-edged throwing knife he kept strapped to his leg. He left his buckskins on the floor, figuring that any hot soapy water that splashed on them had to represent an improvement. Tomorrow he'd figure out a way to give them a thorough airing.

Fargo had just settled into the tub when a deep voice boomed from the other side of the door.

"Everybody out. Now."

"I need ten minutes and a change of water after that," Fargo shouted to the door.

"When I say now, that means now, not sometime next week, asshole."

"When I pay hard cash for a goddamn bath, I figure on getting my money's worth." Things quieted for a moment, so Fargo decided he had made his point. He reached for the pitcher so he could dampen his hair.

The little lull must have been caused by the man outside stepping back so he had enough leverage to kick in the stall door with one tremendous hobnailed thrust. Crackling wood flew toward the tub as the hinges and latch yielded with mournful screeches.

The surly red-bearded man nearly filled the doorway with his broad shoulders. His tree-limb arms looked strong enough to tote ten-gallon buckets to fill baths, but one hand was empty and the other pointed a six-shot Remington at Fargo's forehead, and its hammer was already back. Just about anything might set the gun off.

"Out," he commanded.

"What's your problem?" Fargo countered as he improved his grip on the pitcher.

The big man's grin displayed several missing teeth. "I'm not the one with the problem. You are. Now get out."

"Mind telling me why?"

"I'm the one with the gun here." But the huge man's voice mellowed a bit. "No harm in telling you, though, I reckon. Mr. Abernathy wants to take a bath downstairs. And when Mr. Josiah Abernathy takes a bath, he don't want nobody to disturb his comfort."

"So?"

"So I am his duly hired personal guard, and the easiest way to make sure nobody disturbs him is to clear the place out. An important man like Mr. Abernathy has lots of enemies."

Fargo caught his drift, and saw that the man was getting so exasperated that he wasn't holding the pistol quite so straight anymore. But its muzzle still looked ominous, big enough to crawl down, from where Fargo sat. He wasn't ready to act yet.

"Abernathy?" Fargo wondered aloud, his voice skeptical. "Who the hell is Josiah Abernathy?"

He knew damn well who Josiah Abernathy was. Anybody who'd seen a newspaper in the last four or five years had to be aware of Abernathy, a stock speculator of small morals.

The Remington's muzzle wavered some more as its holder wondered how he could have found someone who had never heard of Josiah Abernathy.

"Josiah Abernathy is about the richest man in the world," Fargo heard. "More to the point, he's my boss, and he wants you somewhere else." The voice was developing an agitated edge.

Fargo nodded agreeably, but used his apparent co-operation as a distraction. It was time to act. Since the pitcher was sitting right before him, between his knees, he couldn't get much leverage. But he could snap his wrists and elbows with enough force to fling a pitcher's worth of hot, soapy water forward, into the big man's astonished eyes.

His instant reflex was to fire the pistol. In the tiny chamber, the explosion left Fargo's ears ringing. But the goon had stumbled back to avoid the water, and the Remington bullet plowed through the back of the chair and plunked against the back wall, so spent that it didn't even penetrate, but dropped to the floor.

Abernathy's bodyguard pawed at his stinging eyes and tried to find Fargo in the haze of powder smoke. The Trailsman heaved another pitcher that way. Still waving the gun, the man lurched forward, only to step atop Fargo's sweat-slicked buckskins.

The waxed plank floor was sopping wet by now, so the buckskins offered about the same footing that a polished ice pond would. Big hobnailed boots slid backward while the huge man tumbled forward, right hand clutching the revolver while he continued to wipe at his face with his ham-sized left.

Aware that he was as safe in the tub as he was anywhere, Fargo remained in place, although he drew his feet up under him so he could spring up fast if necessary.

But first he needed to lean forward. When the flailing gun came near the water, Fargo chopped the massive wrist with his fist. That was only enough to cause a momentary dip, which sent the cylinder into the water for an instant. Then Fargo leaned farther forward, wet soap in hand, and jabbed the bar at his opponent's blinking eyes.

The green orbs started blinking a lot faster after the soap stung their delicate membranes. The man roared. With every bit of control he could muster, he stared at Fargo's rising figure and thumbcocked the revolver. At point-blank range, he had a dead shot at Fargo's back as the Trailsman rose and turned to step out of the tub.

When the hammer fell, the percussion cap did its job with a small bang. But that was all that happened in the moment before Fargo got settled on the chair with his dry Colt.

The big man jerked his revolver around and took another shot at the grinning Trailsman. This time not even the percussion cap went off.

"Stay put for a minute," Fargo commanded, enforcing his words with a menacing motion from the Colt. "Seems to me you disturbed my bath. How do you plan to make it up to me?" Fargo stooped, so that he could reach out and take the man's useless revolver away.

It wasn't quite useless, though. Fargo used it to coldcock the stretched-out hulk. Then he built a gag out of his old socks, which not only stank to high heaven, but felt stiff enough to walk all on their own. He sliced up the bodyguard's leather belt and used some of it to manacle those huge hands behind the man's back. The rest went for hobbles.

Fargo wrapped the towel around himself before he peeked out into the hallway, Colt in hand. As he suspected, the upstairs attendant was long gone. But the Trailsman figured he could find a bucket and the source of the hot water, and then set up in another stall. He still needed a good bath, and one way or another, he was going to get one.

He did. The ruckus downstairs didn't start until the Trailsman was almost dressed, with just his boots to pull on.